Jimmy Gownley's

AMELIA RULES!™

Loosely in Disguise and Frightened

Atheneum Books for Young Readers
New York London Toronto Sydney

Spotlight

VISIT US AT
www.abdopublishing.com

Reinforced library bound edition published in 2011 by Spotlight, a division of the ABDO Group, 8000 West 78th Street, Edina, Minnesota 55439. Spotlight produces high-quality reinforced library bound editions for schools and libraries. Published by agreement with Atheneum Books for Young Readers, an imprint of Simon & Schuster Children's Publishing Division.

Antheneum Books for Young Readers
An imprint of Simon & Schuster Children's Publishing Division
1230 Avenue of the Americans, New York, NY 10020

Printed in the United States of America, Melrose Park, Illinois.
052010
092010
This book contains at least 10% recycled materials.

Library of Congress Cataloging-in-Publication Data

Gownley, Jimmy.
Amelia in Loosely in disguise and frightened / Jimmy Gownley. -- Reinforced library bound ed.
p. cm. -- (Jimmy Gownley's Amelia rules! ; #3)
Summary: On Halloween, when her father cancels their plans, Amelia and her Aunt Tanner throw a party that brings out the little monsters.
ISBN 978-1-59961-789-3
1. Graphic novels. [1. Graphic novels. 2. Halloween--Fiction. 3. Parties--Fiction. 4. Family life--Fiction.] I. Title. II. Title: Loosely in disguise and frightened.
PZ7.7.G69Am 2010
741.5'973--dc22

2010006194

Spotlight

All Spotlight books have reinforced library bindings and are manufactured in the United States of America.

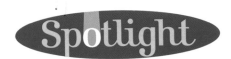

With Love and Thanks
to Mom and Dad...

With appreciation for
the Vision and Faith of
Joe, John, Jerry, and Bill...

And with gratitude for
the Patience and Friendship
of Michael...

This book is dedicated with love...
for Karen.

J-GN
AMELIA RULES
399-7205

Loosely in
Disguise and
Frightened

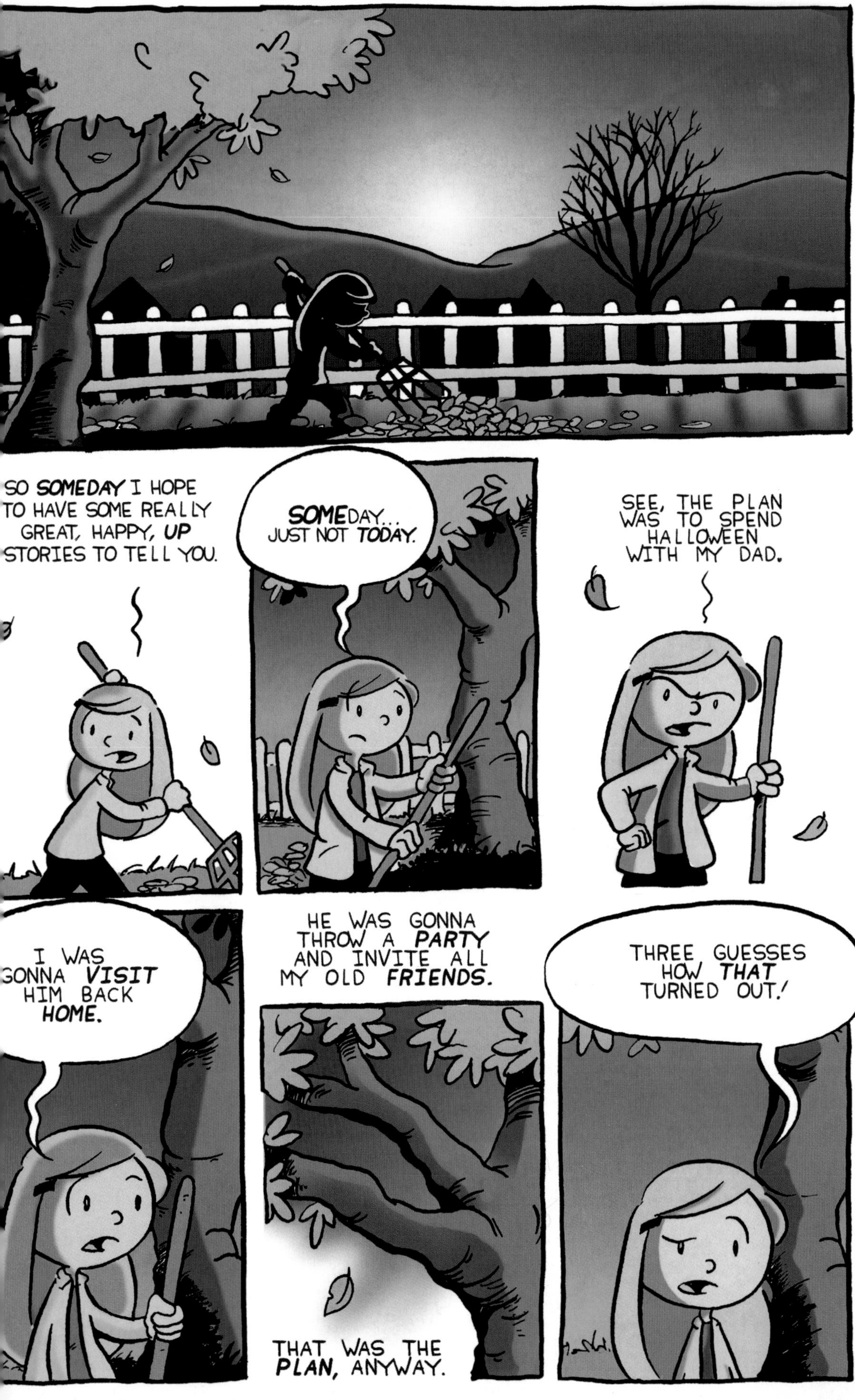
SO SOMEDAY I HOPE TO HAVE SOME REALLY GREAT, HAPPY, UP STORIES TO TELL YOU.
SOMEDAY... JUST NOT TODAY.
SEE, THE PLAN WAS TO SPEND HALLOWEEN WITH MY DAD.
I WAS GONNA VISIT HIM BACK HOME.
HE WAS GONNA THROW A PARTY AND INVITE ALL MY OLD FRIENDS.
THAT WAS THE PLAN, ANYWAY.
THREE GUESSES HOW THAT TURNED OUT!

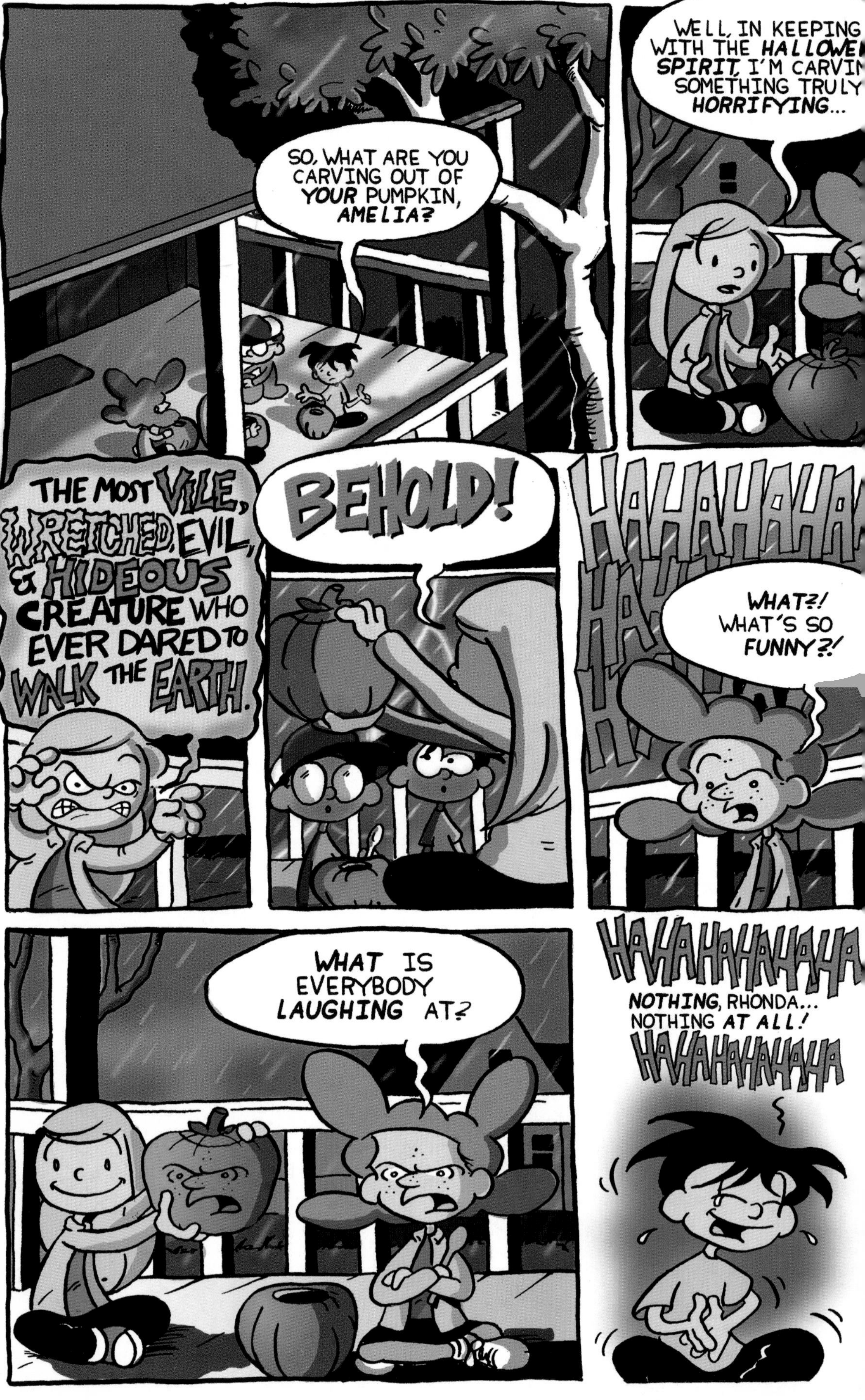

SO, WHAT ARE YOU CARVING OUT OF YOUR PUMPKIN, AMELIA?
WELL, IN KEEPING WITH THE HALLOWE SPIRIT, I'M CARVIN SOMETHING TRULY HORRIFYING...
THE MOST VILE, WRETCHED, EVIL, & HIDEOUS CREATURE WHO EVER DARED TO WALK THE EARTH.
BEHOLD!
HAHAHAHAHA
WHAT?! WHAT'S SO FUNNY?!
WHAT IS EVERYBODY LAUGHING AT?
HAHAHAHAHAHAHA
NOTHING, RHONDA... NOTHING AT ALL!
HAHAHAHAHAHA

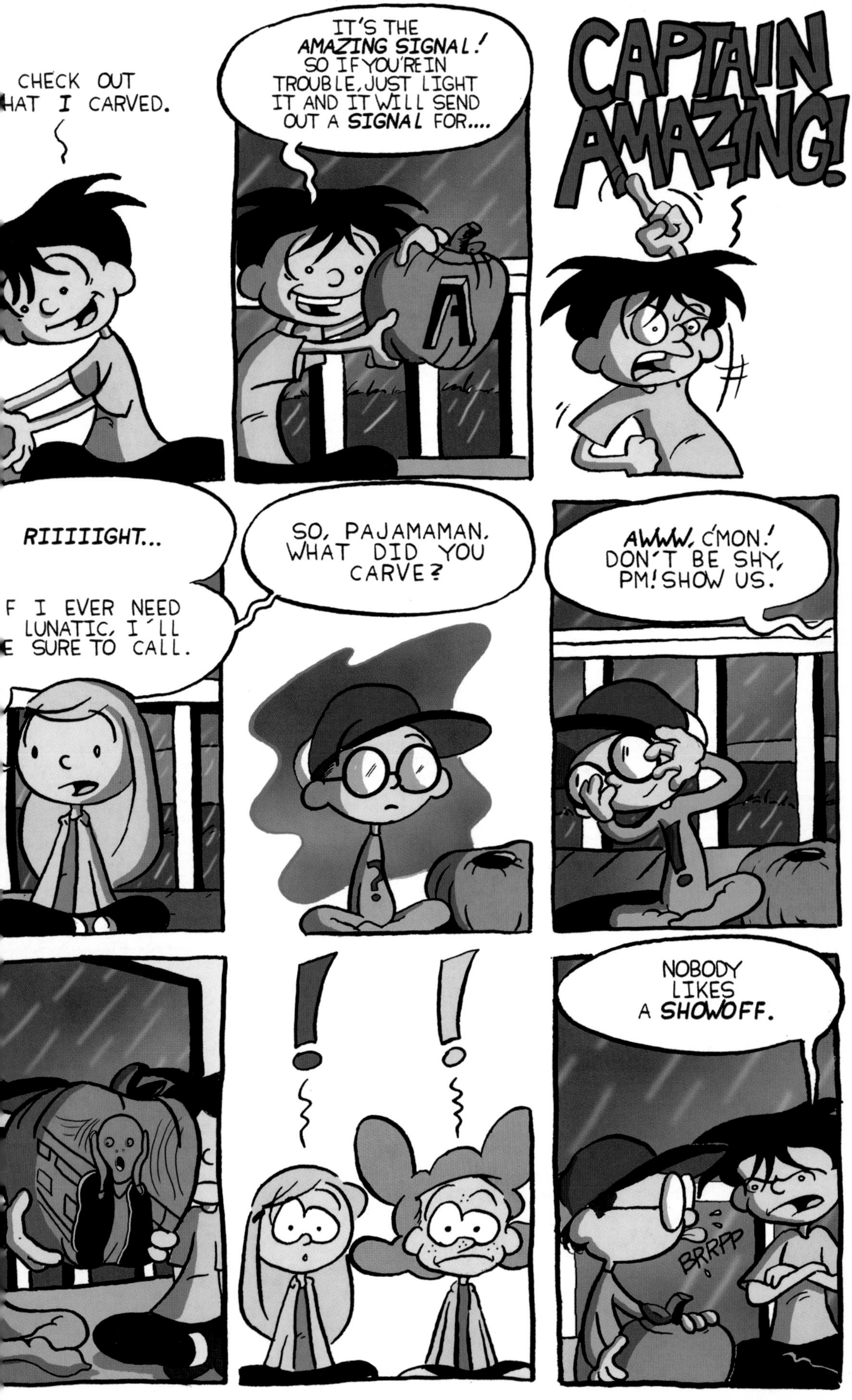
CHECK OUT
HAT I CARVED.
IT'S THE AMAZING SIGNAL! SO IF YOU'RE IN TROUBLE, JUST LIGHT IT AND IT WILL SEND OUT A SIGNAL FOR....
CAPTAIN AMAZING!
RIIIIIGHT...
F I EVER NEED LUNATIC, I'LL E SURE TO CALL.
SO, PAJAMAMAN. WHAT DID YOU CARVE?
AWWW, C'MON! DON'T BE SHY, PM! SHOW US.
!
!
NOBODY LIKES A SHOWOFF.
BRRPP

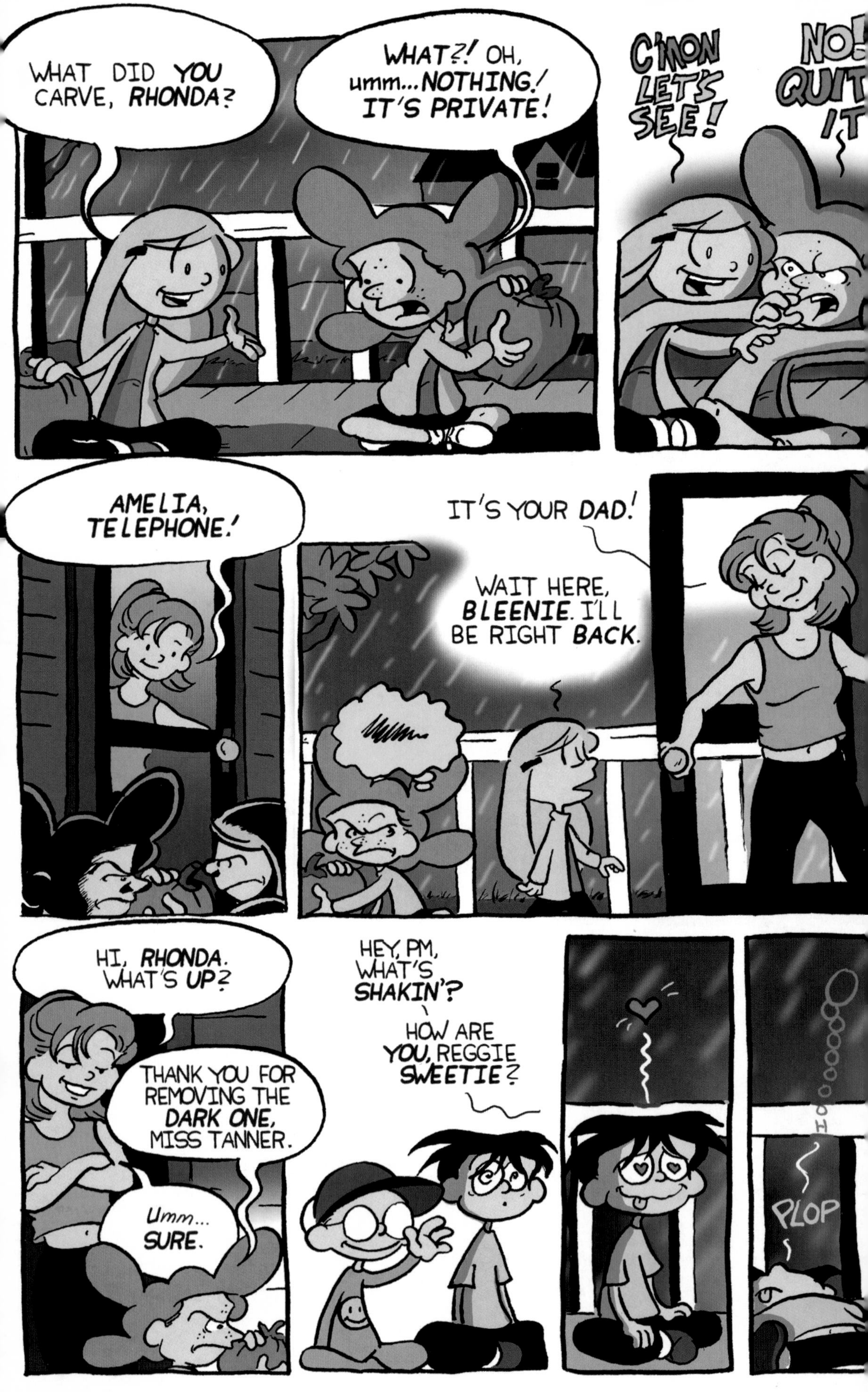
WHAT DID YOU CARVE, RHONDA?
WHAT?! OH, umm... NOTHING! IT'S PRIVATE!
C'MON LET'S SEE!
NO! QUIT IT
AMELIA, TELEPHONE!
IT'S YOUR DAD!
WAIT HERE, BLEENIE. I'LL BE RIGHT BACK.
HI, RHONDA. WHAT'S UP?
THANK YOU FOR REMOVING THE DARK ONE, MISS TANNER.
Umm... SURE.
HEY, PM, WHAT'S SHAKIN'?
HOW ARE YOU, REGGIE SWEETIE?
PLOP

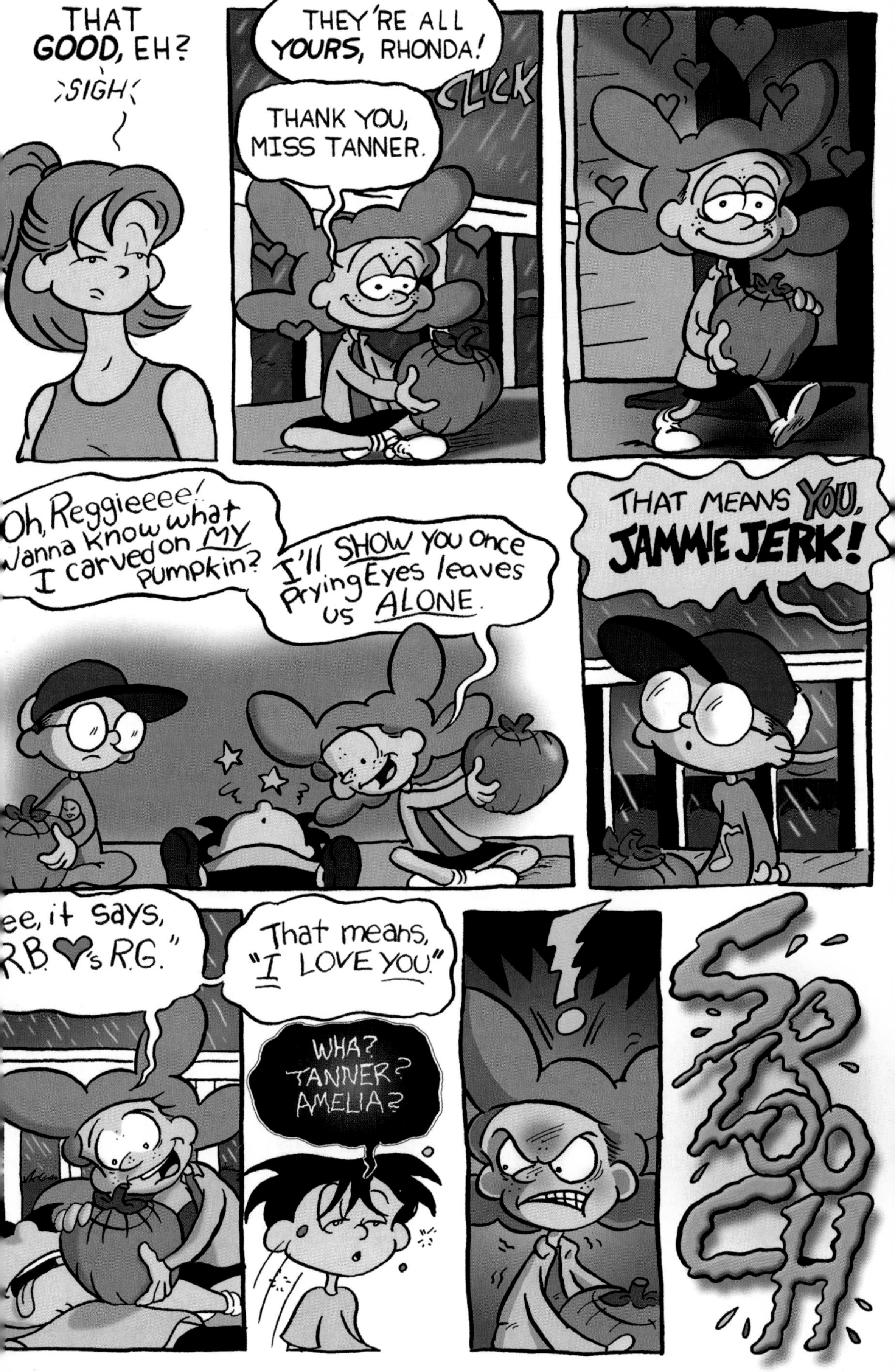

THAT GOOD, EH?
>SIGH<
THEY'RE ALL YOURS, RHONDA!
CLICK
THANK YOU, MISS TANNER.
Oh, Reggieeee! Wanna know what I carved on MY pumpkin?
I'll SHOW you once Prying Eyes leaves us ALONE.
THAT MEANS YOU, JAMMIE JERK!
ee, it says, R.B. ♥'s R.G."
That means, "I LOVE YOU."
WHA? TANNER? AMELIA?
SPLOOSH

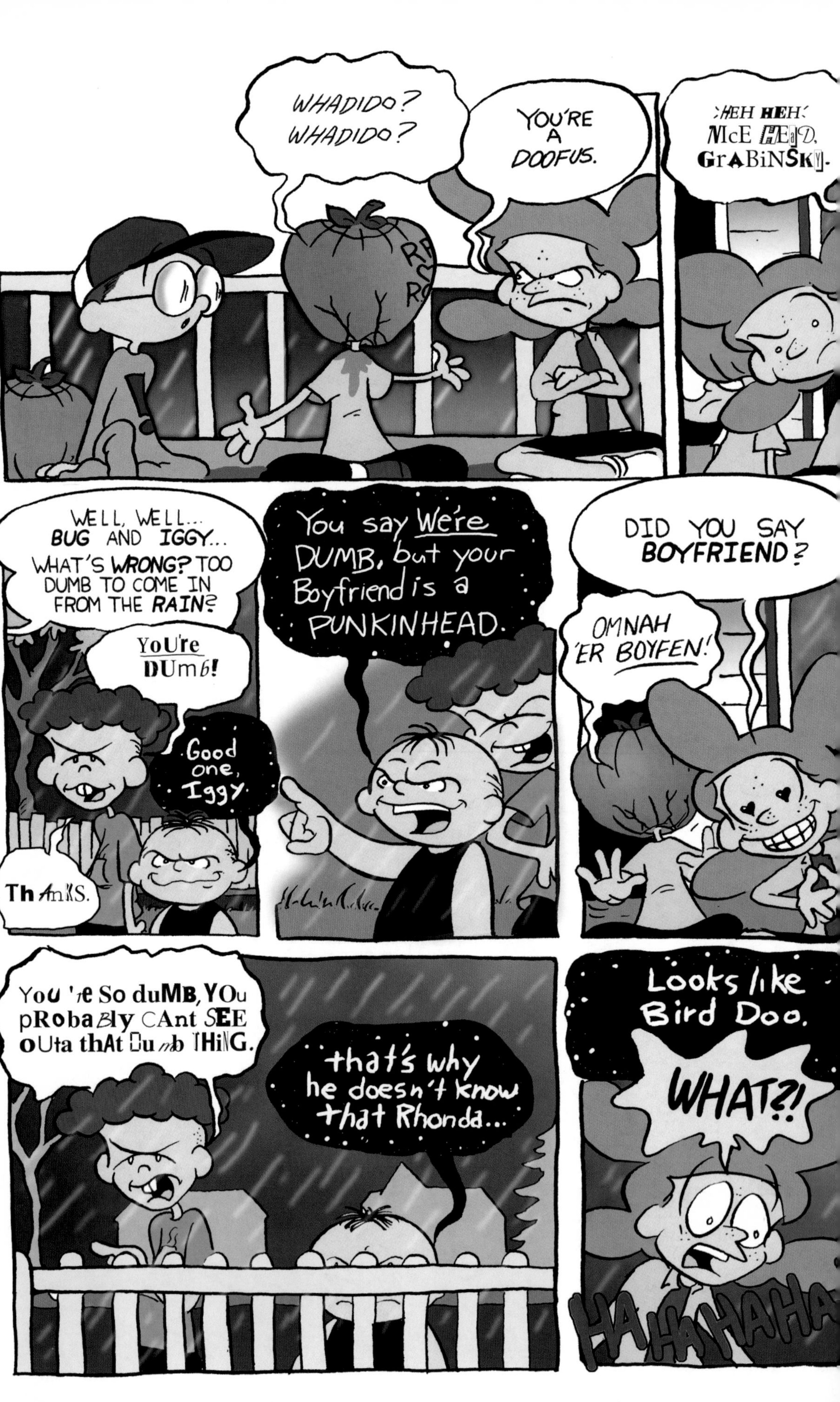
WHADIDO? WHADIDO?
YOU'RE A DOOFUS.
HEH HEH. MCE HEAD, GRABINSKY.
WELL, WELL... BUG AND IGGY... WHAT'S WRONG? TOO DUMB TO COME IN FROM THE RAIN?
YoU're DUmb!
Good one, Iggy.
ThAnKS.
You say We're DUMB, but your Boyfriend is a PUNKINHEAD.
DID YOU SAY BOYFRIEND?
OMNAH 'ER BOYFEN!
YoU 're So duMB, YOu pRobaBly CAnt SEE oUta thAt DUmb THiNG.
that's why he doesn't know that Rhonda...
Looks like Bird Doo.
WHAT?!
HAHAHAHAHA

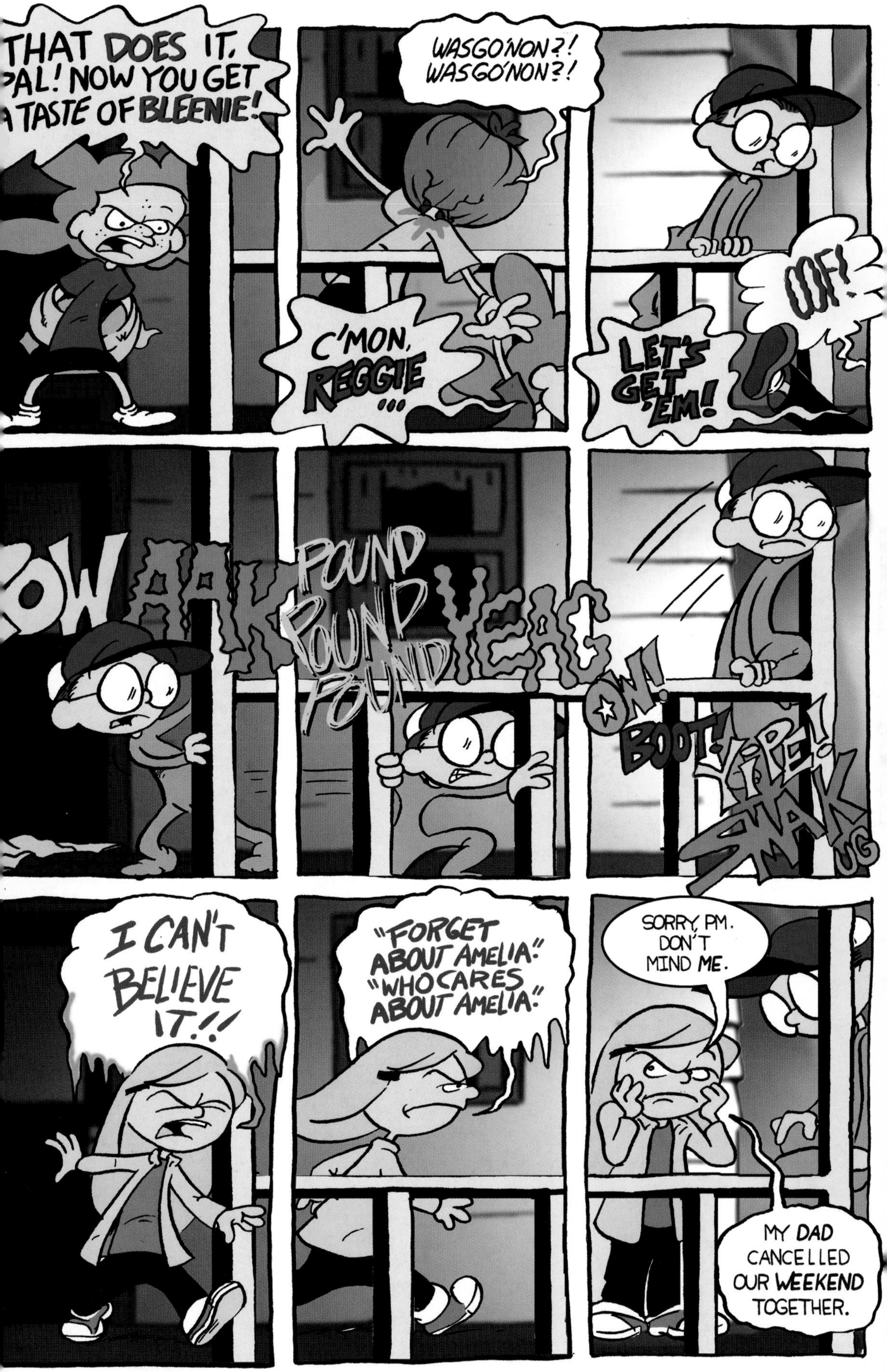
THAT DOES IT, PAL! NOW YOU GET A TASTE OF BLEENIE!
WASGO'NON?! WASGO'NON?!
C'MON, REGGIE...
LET'S GET 'EM!
OOF!
OW
AAK
POUND POUND POUND
YEAG
BOOT!
YIPE!
SMAK
UG
I CAN'T BELIEVE IT!!
"FORGET ABOUT AMELIA." "WHO CARES ABOUT AMELIA."
SORRY, PM. DON'T MIND ME.
MY DAD CANCELLED OUR WEEKEND TOGETHER.

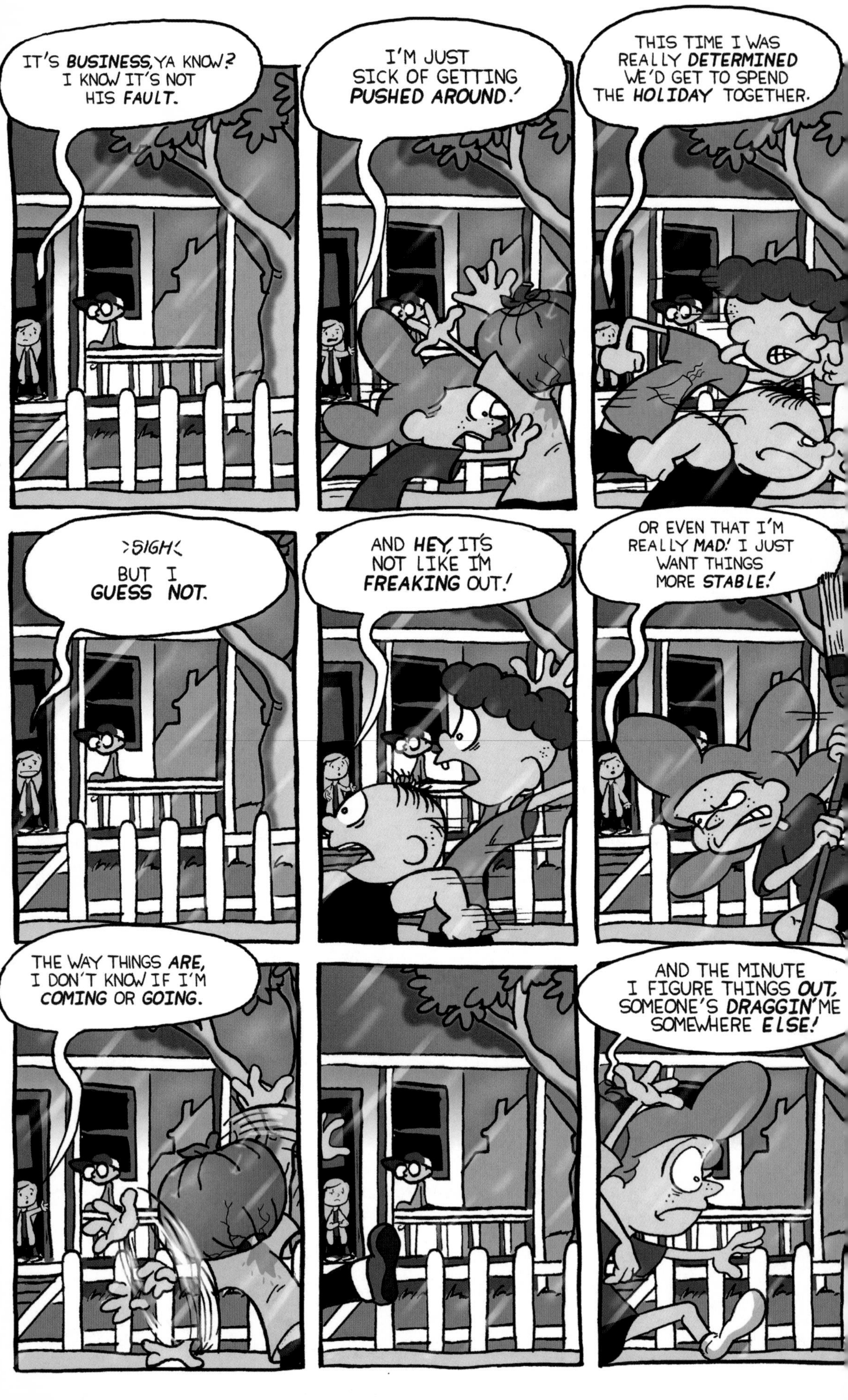

IT'S BUSINESS, YA KNOW? I KNOW IT'S NOT HIS FAULT.
I'M JUST SICK OF GETTING PUSHED AROUND!
THIS TIME I WAS REALLY DETERMINED WE'D GET TO SPEND THE HOLIDAY TOGETHER.
>SIGH< BUT I GUESS NOT.
AND HEY, IT'S NOT LIKE I'M FREAKING OUT!
OR EVEN THAT I'M REALLY MAD! I JUST WANT THINGS MORE STABLE!
THE WAY THINGS ARE, I DON'T KNOW IF I'M COMING OR GOING.
AND THE MINUTE I FIGURE THINGS OUT, SOMEONE'S DRAGGIN' ME SOMEWHERE ELSE!

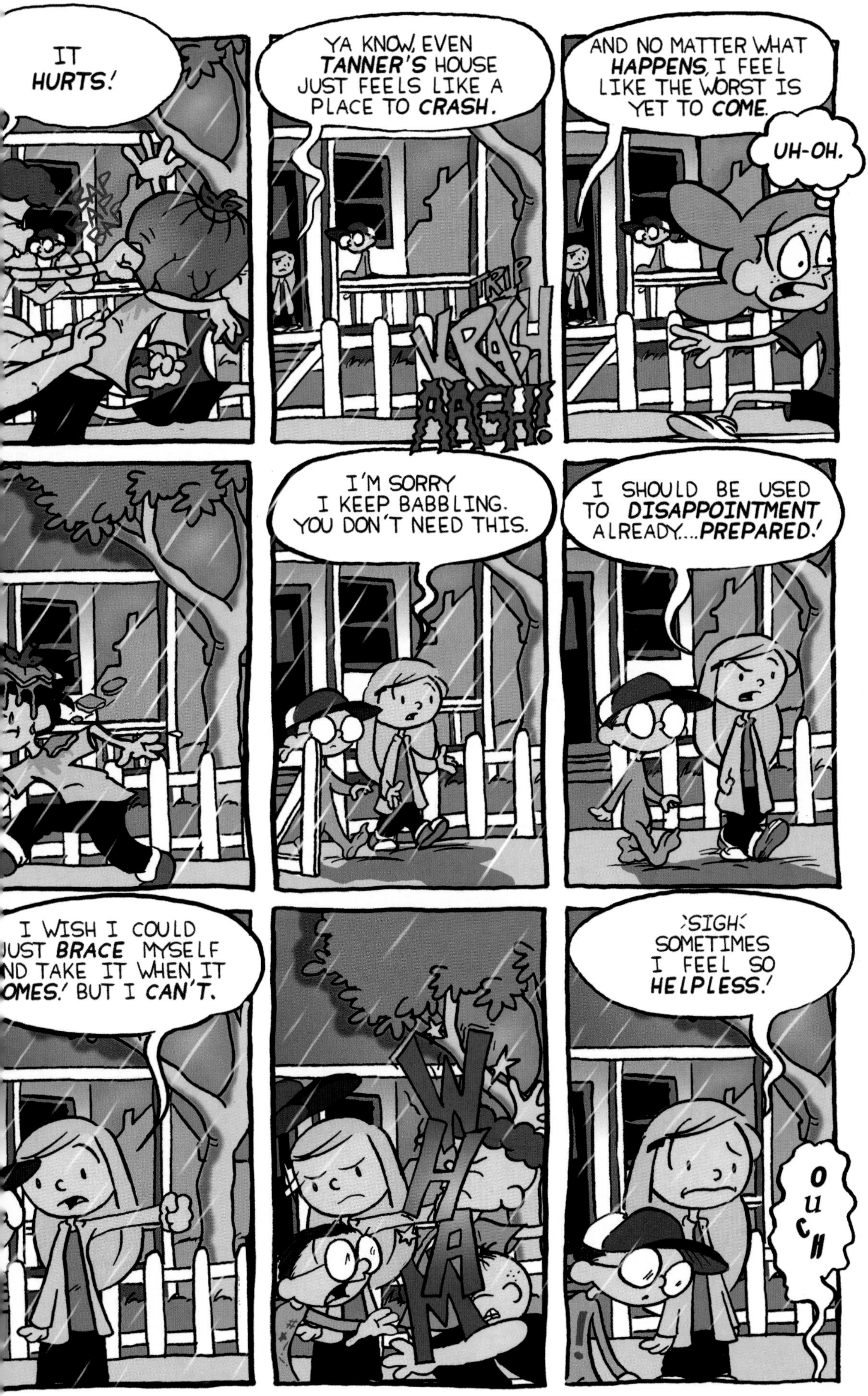
IT HURTS!
YA KNOW, EVEN TANNER'S HOUSE JUST FEELS LIKE A PLACE TO CRASH.
TRIP
KRASH
AAGH!
AND NO MATTER WHAT HAPPENS, I FEEL LIKE THE WORST IS YET TO COME.
UH-OH.
I'M SORRY I KEEP BABBLING. YOU DON'T NEED THIS.
I SHOULD BE USED TO DISAPPOINTMENT ALREADY.... PREPARED!
I WISH I COULD UST BRACE MYSELF ND TAKE IT WHEN IT OMES! BUT I CAN'T.
WHAM
›SIGH‹ SOMETIMES I FEEL SO HELPLESS!
OUCH

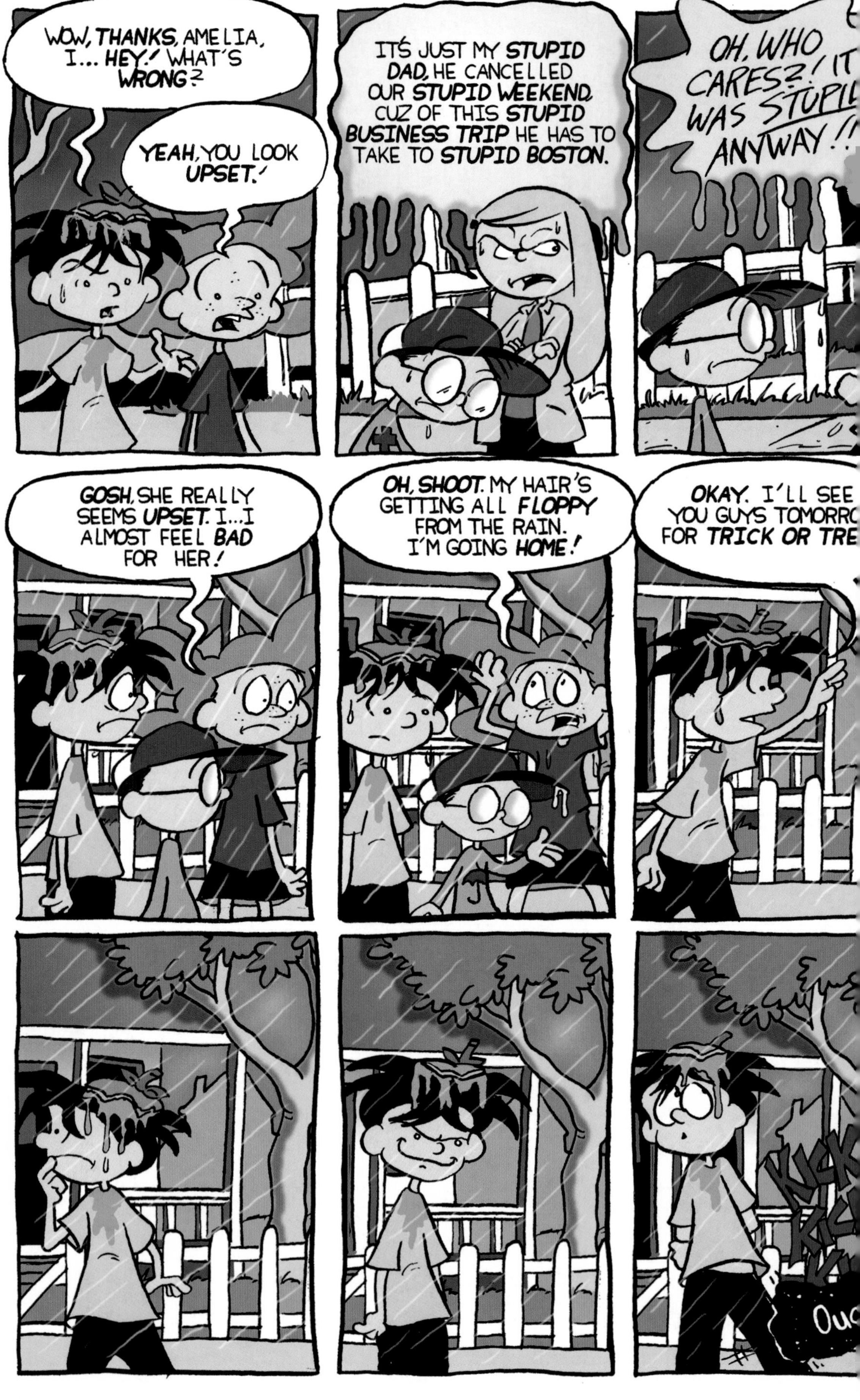
WOW, THANKS, AMELIA, I... HEY! WHAT'S WRONG?
YEAH, YOU LOOK UPSET!
IT'S JUST MY STUPID DAD, HE CANCELLED OUR STUPID WEEKEND, CUZ OF THIS STUPID BUSINESS TRIP HE HAS TO TAKE TO STUPID BOSTON.
OH, WHO CARES?! IT WAS STUPI
ANYWAY!!
GOSH, SHE REALLY SEEMS UPSET. I...I ALMOST FEEL BAD FOR HER!
OH, SHOOT. MY HAIR'S GETTING ALL FLOPPY FROM THE RAIN. I'M GOING HOME!
OKAY. I'LL SEE YOU GUYS TOMORRO
FOR TRICK OR TRE

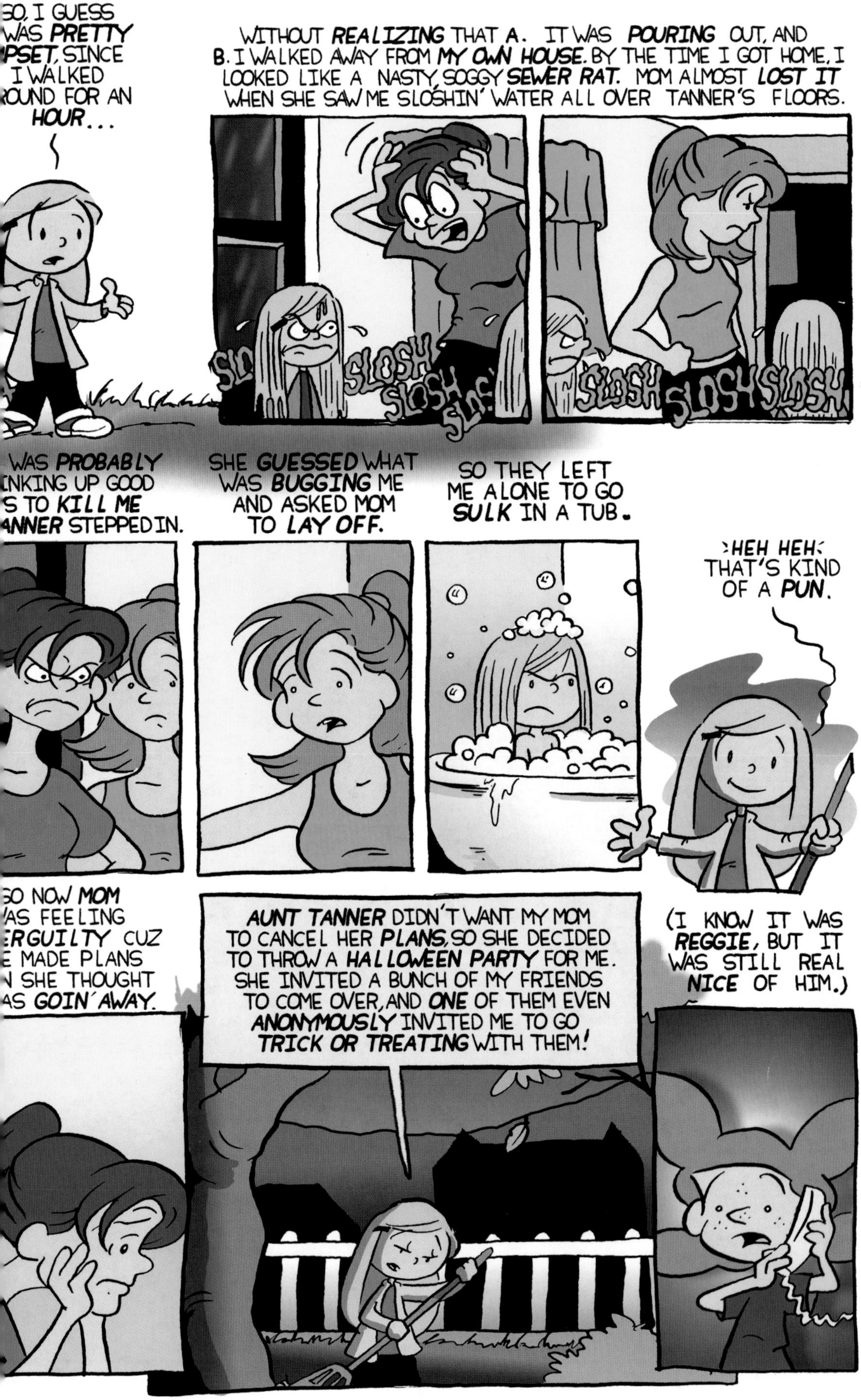

SO, I GUESS WAS PRETTY PSET, SINCE I WALKED ROUND FOR AN HOUR...
WITHOUT REALIZING THAT A. IT WAS POURING OUT, AND B. I WALKED AWAY FROM MY OWN HOUSE. BY THE TIME I GOT HOME, I LOOKED LIKE A NASTY, SOGGY SEWER RAT. MOM ALMOST LOST IT WHEN SHE SAW ME SLOSHIN' WATER ALL OVER TANNER'S FLOORS.
SLOSH
SLOSH
SLOSH
SLOSH
SLOSH
SLOSH
WAS PROBABLY INKING UP GOOD S TO KILL ME ANNER STEPPED IN.
SHE GUESSED WHAT WAS BUGGING ME AND ASKED MOM TO LAY OFF.
SO THEY LEFT ME ALONE TO GO SULK IN A TUB.
HEH HEH THAT'S KIND OF A PUN.
SO NOW MOM AS FEELING ERGUILTY CUZ E MADE PLANS N SHE THOUGHT AS GOIN' AWAY.
AUNT TANNER DIDN'T WANT MY MOM TO CANCEL HER PLANS, SO SHE DECIDED TO THROW A HALLOWEEN PARTY FOR ME. SHE INVITED A BUNCH OF MY FRIENDS TO COME OVER, AND ONE OF THEM EVEN ANONYMOUSLY INVITED ME TO GO TRICK OR TREATING WITH THEM!
(I KNOW IT WAS REGGIE, BUT IT WAS STILL REAL NICE OF HIM.)

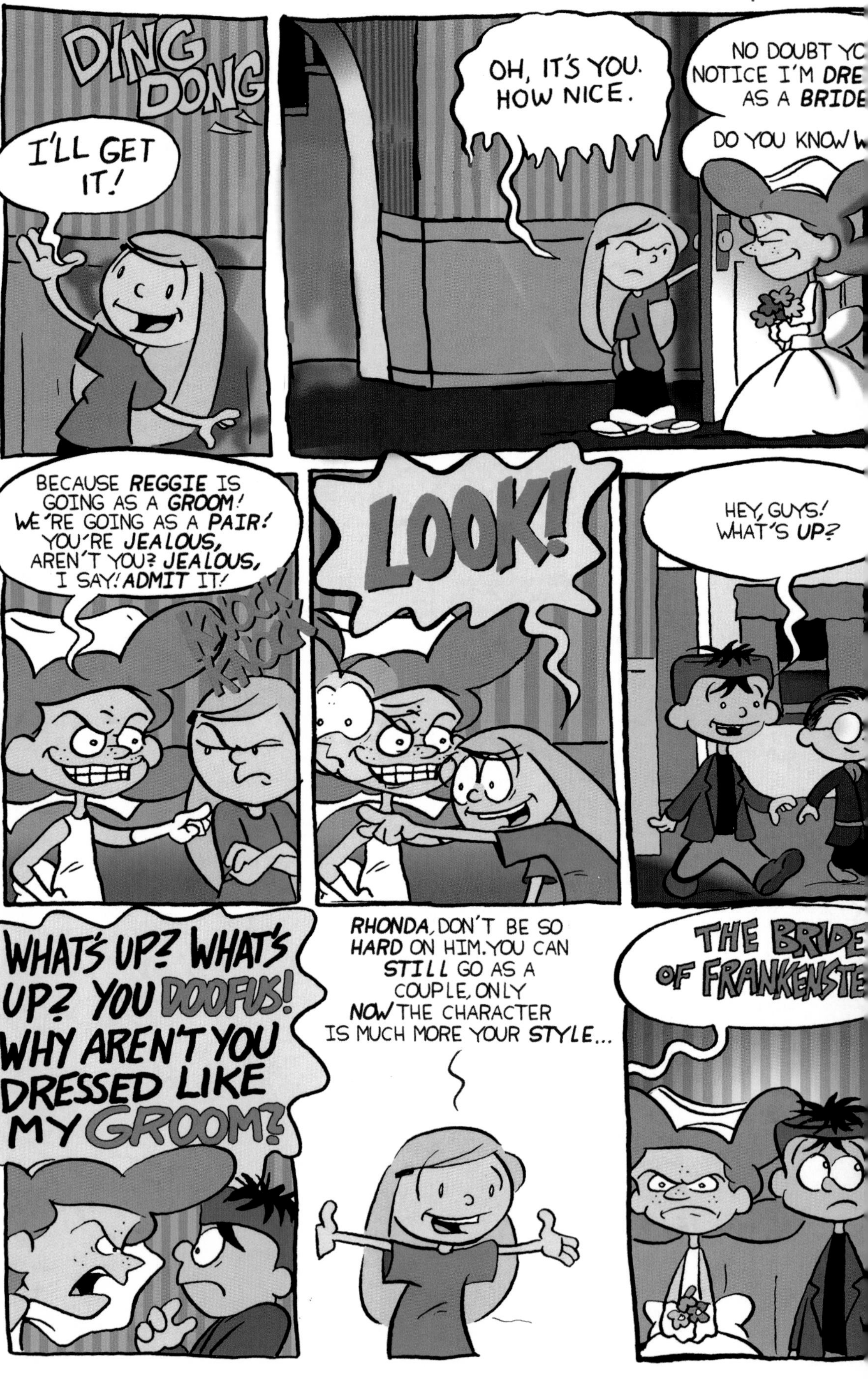
DING DONG
I'LL GET IT!
OH, IT'S YOU. HOW NICE.
NO DOUBT YO
NOTICE I'M DRE
AS A BRIDE
DO YOU KNOW W
BECAUSE REGGIE IS GOING AS A GROOM! WE'RE GOING AS A PAIR! YOU'RE JEALOUS, AREN'T YOU? JEALOUS, I SAY! ADMIT IT!
KNOCK KNOCK
LOOK!
HEY, GUYS! WHAT'S UP?
WHAT'S UP? WHAT'S UP? YOU DOOFUS! WHY AREN'T YOU DRESSED LIKE MY GROOM?
RHONDA, DON'T BE SO HARD ON HIM. YOU CAN STILL GO AS A COUPLE, ONLY NOW THE CHARACTER IS MUCH MORE YOUR STYLE...
THE BRIDE
OF FRANKENSTE

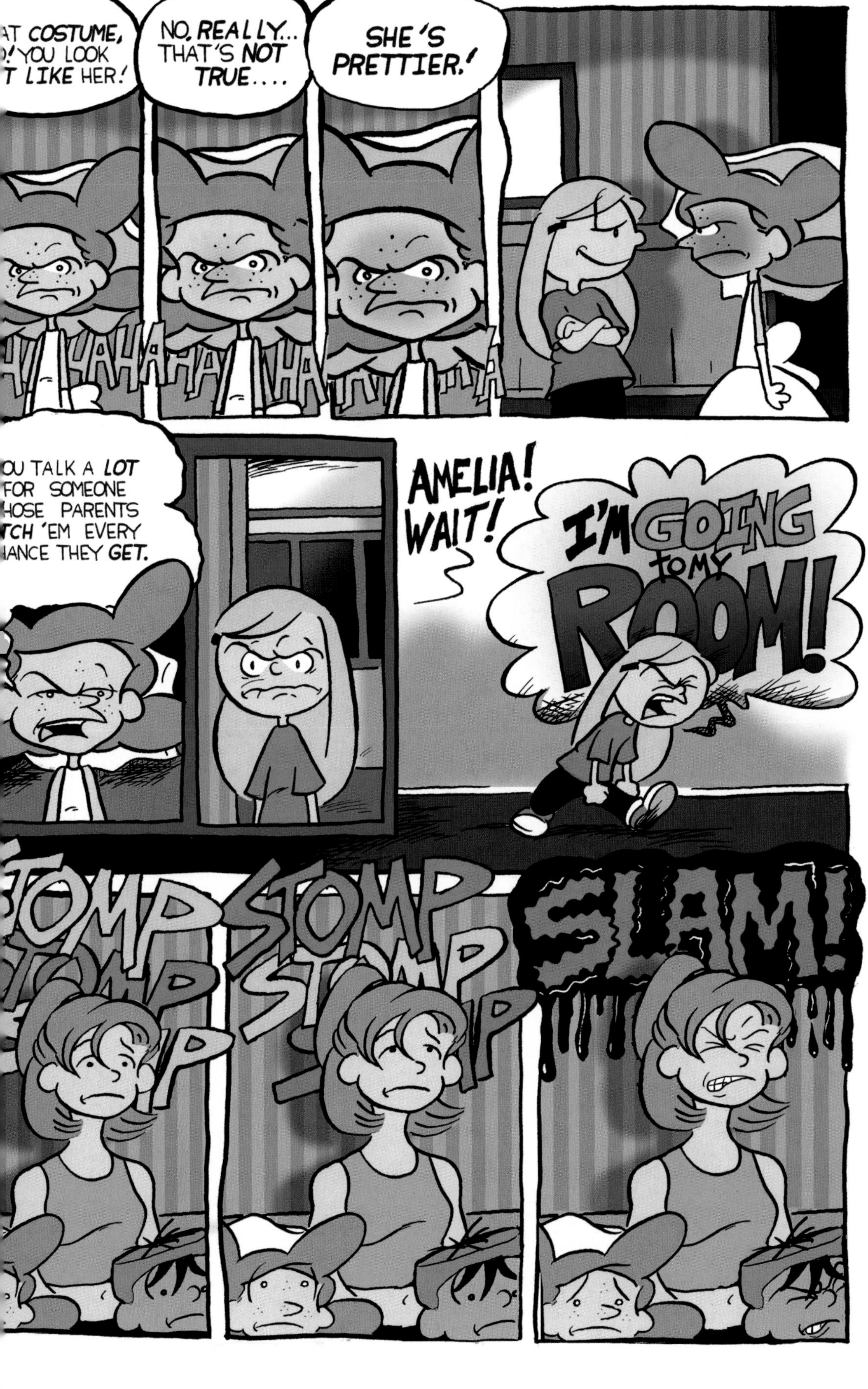

AT COSTUME, YOU LOOK T LIKE HER!
NO, REALLY... THAT'S NOT TRUE....
SHE'S PRETTIER!
OU TALK A LOT FOR SOMEONE HOSE PARENTS TCH 'EM EVERY ANCE THEY GET.
AMELIA! WAIT!
I'M GOING to MY ROOM!
STOMP
STOMP
STOMP
SLAM!

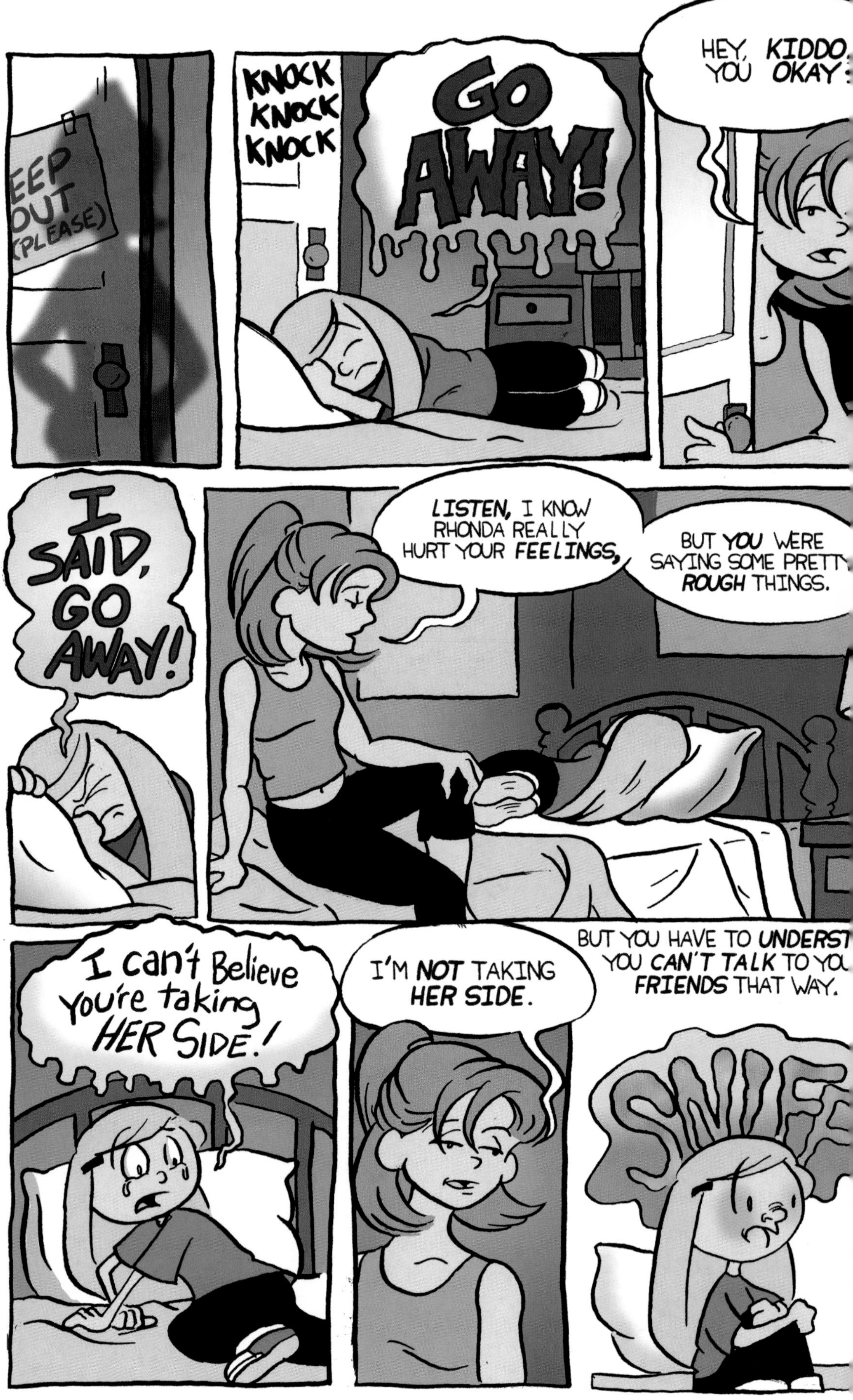

EEP
OUT
(PLEASE)
KNOCK KNOCK KNOCK
GO AWAY!
HEY, KIDDO. YOU OKAY?
I SAID, GO AWAY!
LISTEN, I KNOW RHONDA REALLY HURT YOUR FEELINGS,
BUT YOU WERE SAYING SOME PRETTY ROUGH THINGS.
I can't Believe you're taking HER SIDE!
I'M NOT TAKING HER SIDE.
BUT YOU HAVE TO UNDERST
YOU CAN'T TALK TO YOU
FRIENDS THAT WAY.
SNIFF

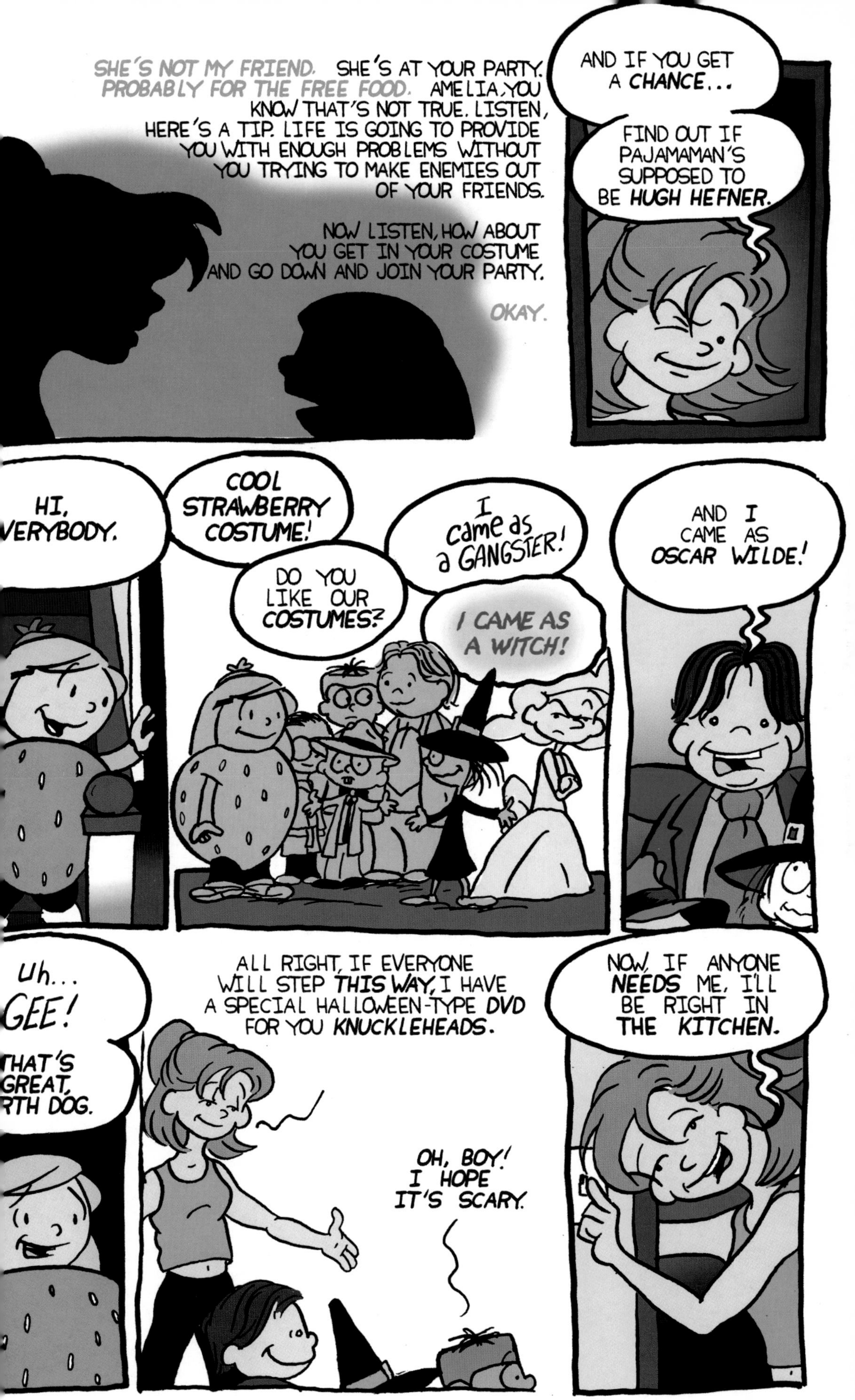
SHE'S NOT MY FRIEND. SHE'S AT YOUR PARTY. PROBABLY FOR THE FREE FOOD. AMELIA, YOU KNOW THAT'S NOT TRUE. LISTEN, HERE'S A TIP. LIFE IS GOING TO PROVIDE YOU WITH ENOUGH PROBLEMS WITHOUT YOU TRYING TO MAKE ENEMIES OUT OF YOUR FRIENDS.
NOW LISTEN, HOW ABOUT YOU GET IN YOUR COSTUME AND GO DOWN AND JOIN YOUR PARTY.
OKAY.
AND IF YOU GET A CHANCE...
FIND OUT IF PAJAMAMAN'S SUPPOSED TO BE HUGH HEFNER.
HI, VERYBODY.
COOL STRAWBERRY COSTUME!
DO YOU LIKE OUR COSTUMES?
I came as a GANGSTER!
I CAME AS A WITCH!
AND I CAME AS OSCAR WILDE!
Uh... GEE!
THAT'S GREAT, RTH DOG.
ALL RIGHT, IF EVERYONE WILL STEP THIS WAY, I HAVE A SPECIAL HALLOWEEN-TYPE DVD FOR YOU KNUCKLEHEADS.
OH, BOY! I HOPE IT'S SCARY.
NOW, IF ANYONE NEEDS ME, I'LL BE RIGHT IN THE KITCHEN.

OH DEAR. I HOPE THIS ISN'T TOO SCARY!
T'sk- Dames!
I CAN BARELY SEE OVER MY BERRY!
SHH! IT'S ON!
ZOMB GOR PART2
SAY, BABY, YOU DON'T MIND IF WE WALK THROUGH THIS OLD CEMETERY, DO YA?
YOU HAVE SOME NERVE, NOT COMING AS MY GROOM!
I JUST THOUGHT IT WAS A STUPID IDEA! BESIDES, EVERYONE WOULD MAKE FUN OF ME!
WHY IF I DIDN'T KN BETTER I'D YOU WER
SOMEDAY, YOU'RE GONN LOSE ME, REGG GRABINSKY
WILL YOU SHUT UP! WE'RE TRYING TO WATCH THE MOVIE!
GROAN
NOW, BABY... WHY WOULD...
WAIT! LOOK OUT BEHIND YOU!

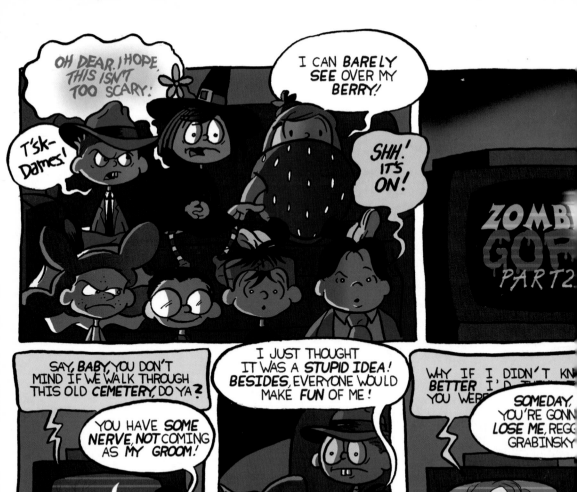

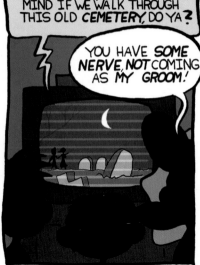

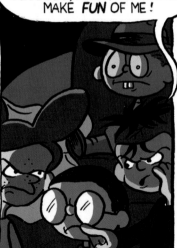

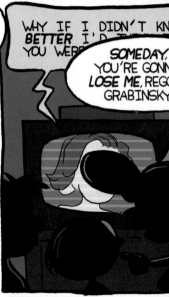

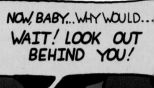

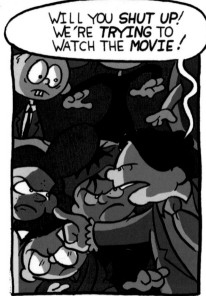

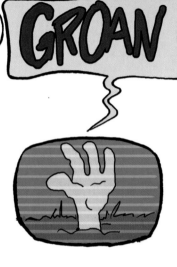

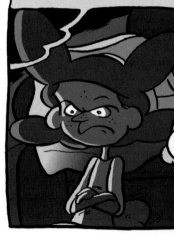

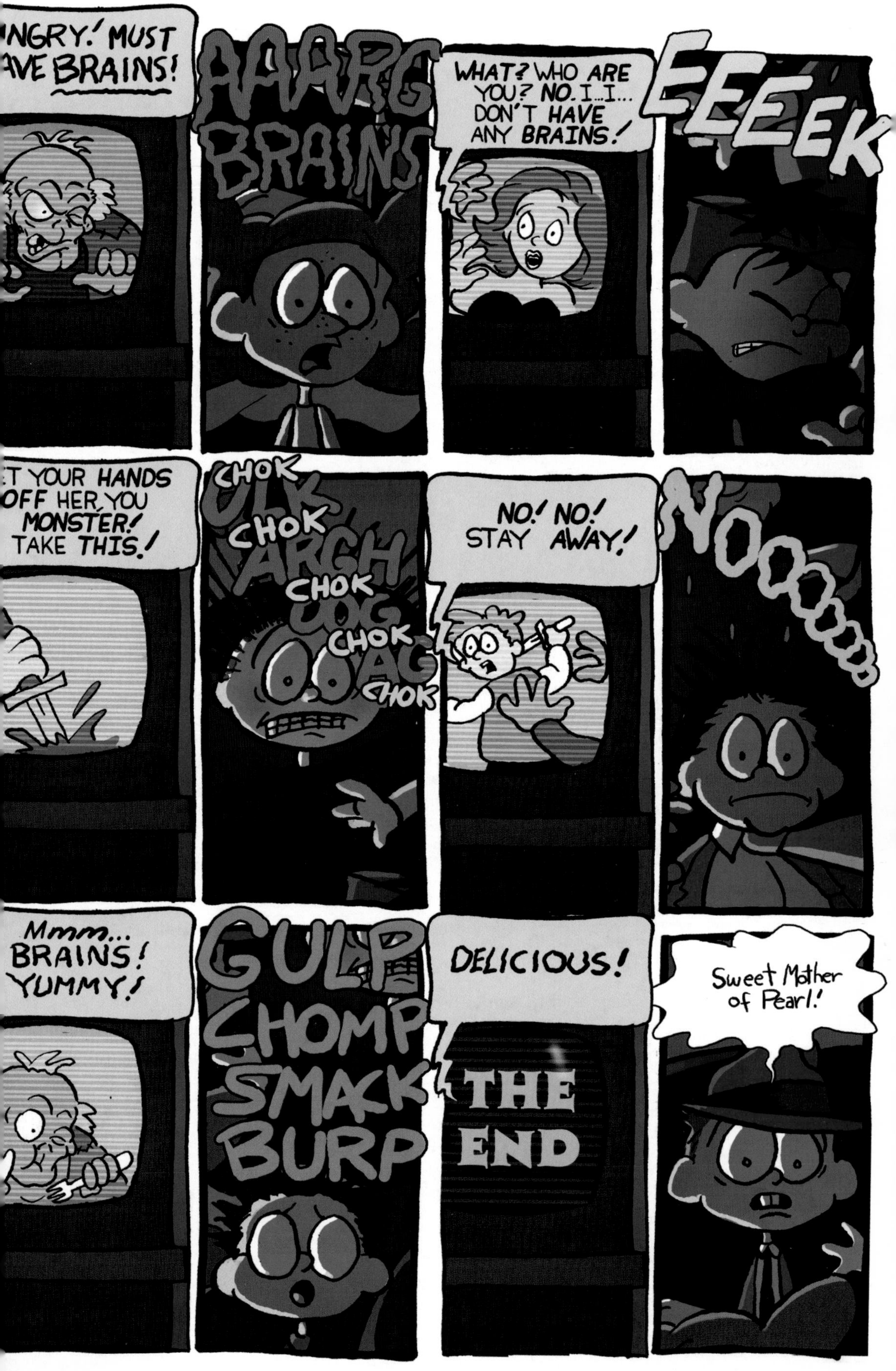
NGRY! MUST
AVE BRAINS!
AAARG
BRAINS
WHAT? WHO ARE YOU? NO. I...I... DON'T HAVE ANY BRAINS!
EEEEEK
T YOUR HANDS OFF HER, YOU MONSTER! TAKE THIS!
CHOK
CHOK
ARGH
CHOK
CHOK
AG
CHOK
NO! NO! STAY AWAY!
NOOOOOO
Mmm... BRAINS! YUMMY!
GULP
CHOMP
SMACK
BURP
DELICIOUS!
THE END
Sweet Mother of Pearl!

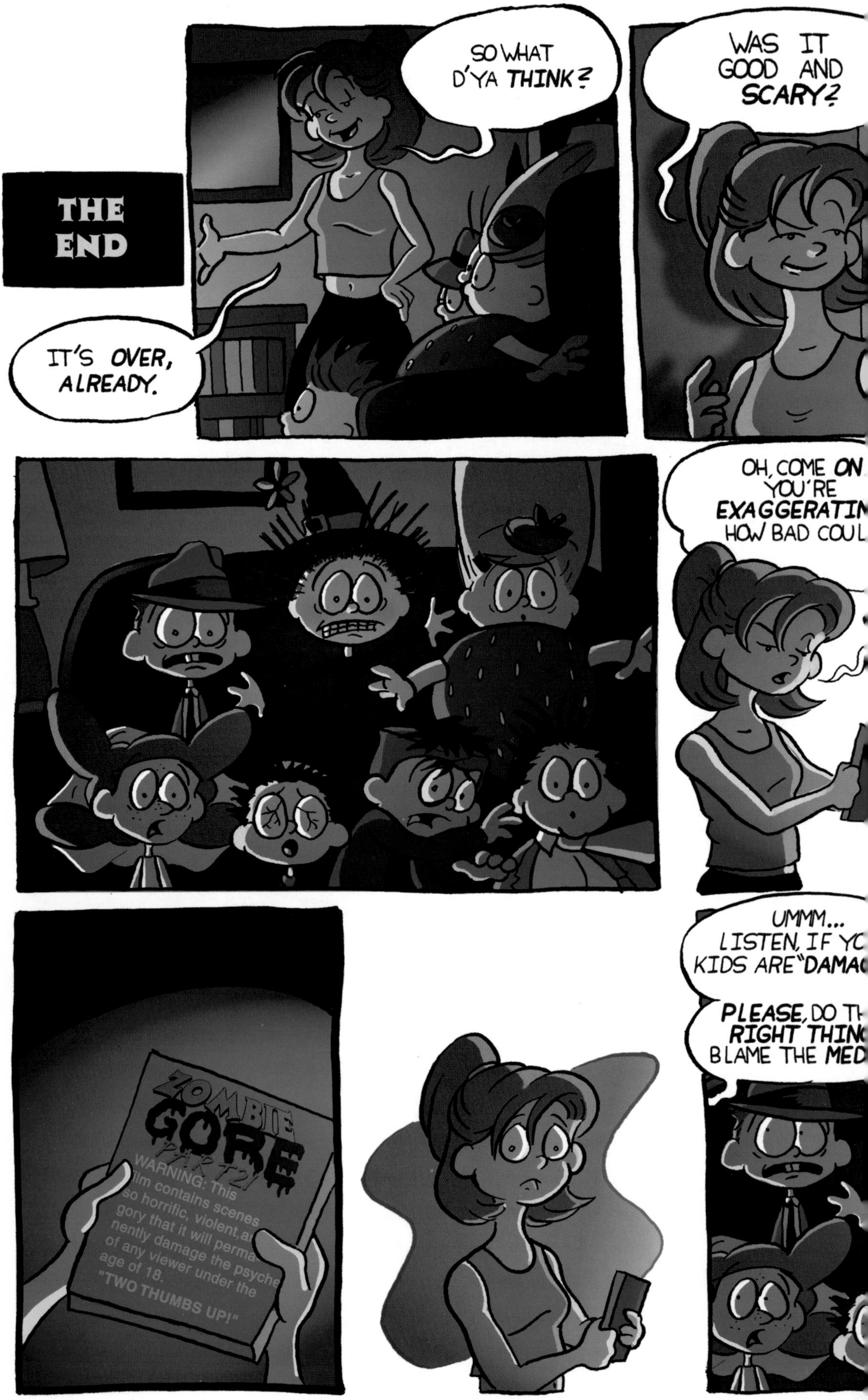
THE END
IT'S OVER, ALREADY.
SO WHAT D'YA THINK?
WAS IT GOOD AND SCARY?
OH, COME ON
YOU'RE
EXAGGERATIN
HOW BAD COUL
ZOMBIE GORE PART 21
WARNING: This film contains scenes so horrific, violent, ar gory that it will perma- nently damage the psyche of any viewer under the age of 18.
"TWO THUMBS UP!"
UMMM... LISTEN, IF YO KIDS ARE "DAMA
PLEASE, DO TH RIGHT THIN BLAME THE MED

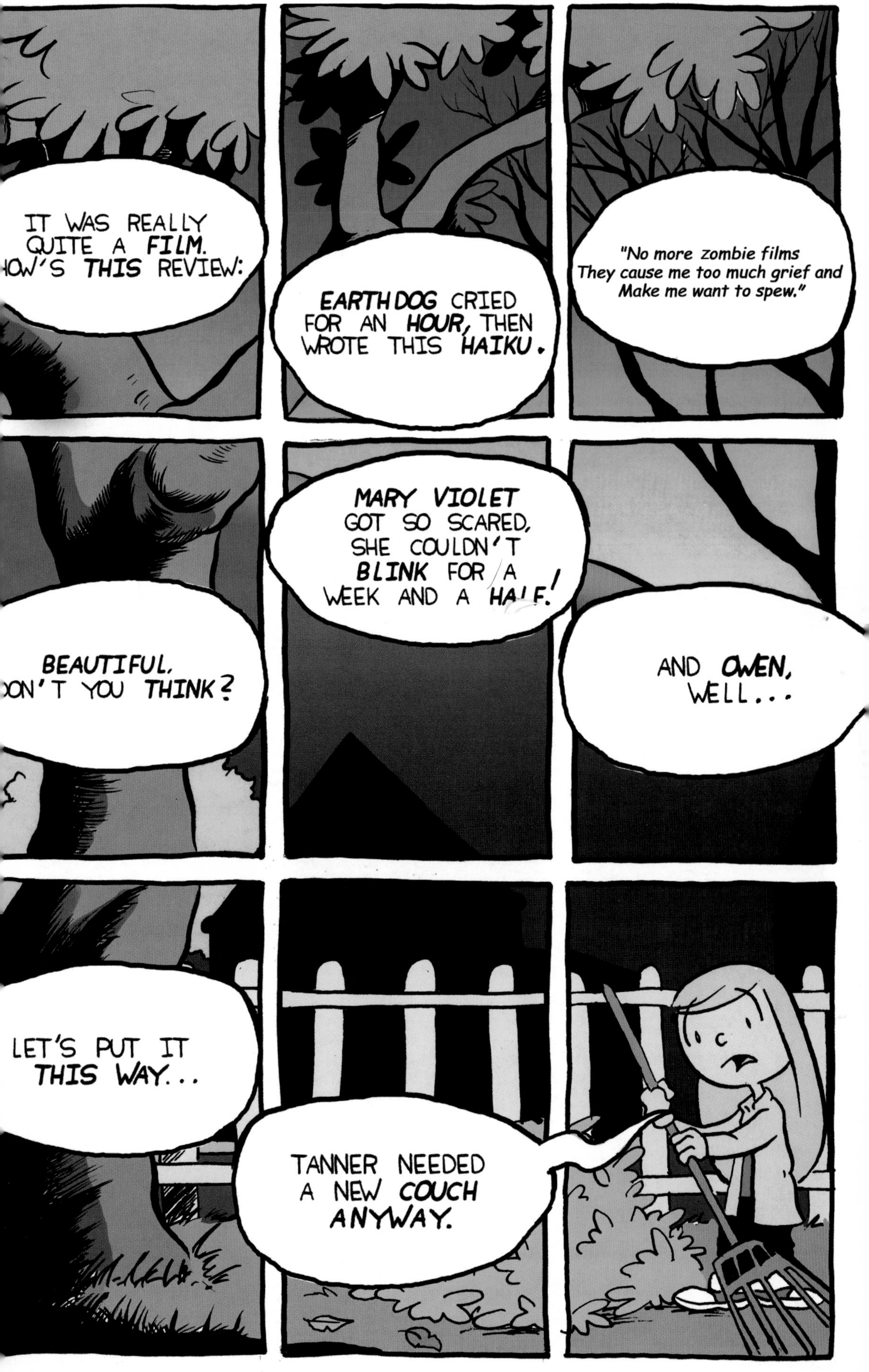
IT WAS REALLY QUITE A FILM. HOW'S THIS REVIEW:
EARTHDOG CRIED FOR AN HOUR, THEN WROTE THIS HAIKU.
"No more zombie films
They cause me too much grief and
Make me want to spew."
BEAUTIFUL, DON'T YOU THINK?
MARY VIOLET GOT SO SCARED, SHE COULDN'T BLINK FOR A WEEK AND A HALF!
AND OWEN, WELL...
LET'S PUT IT THIS WAY...
TANNER NEEDED A NEW COUCH ANYWAY.

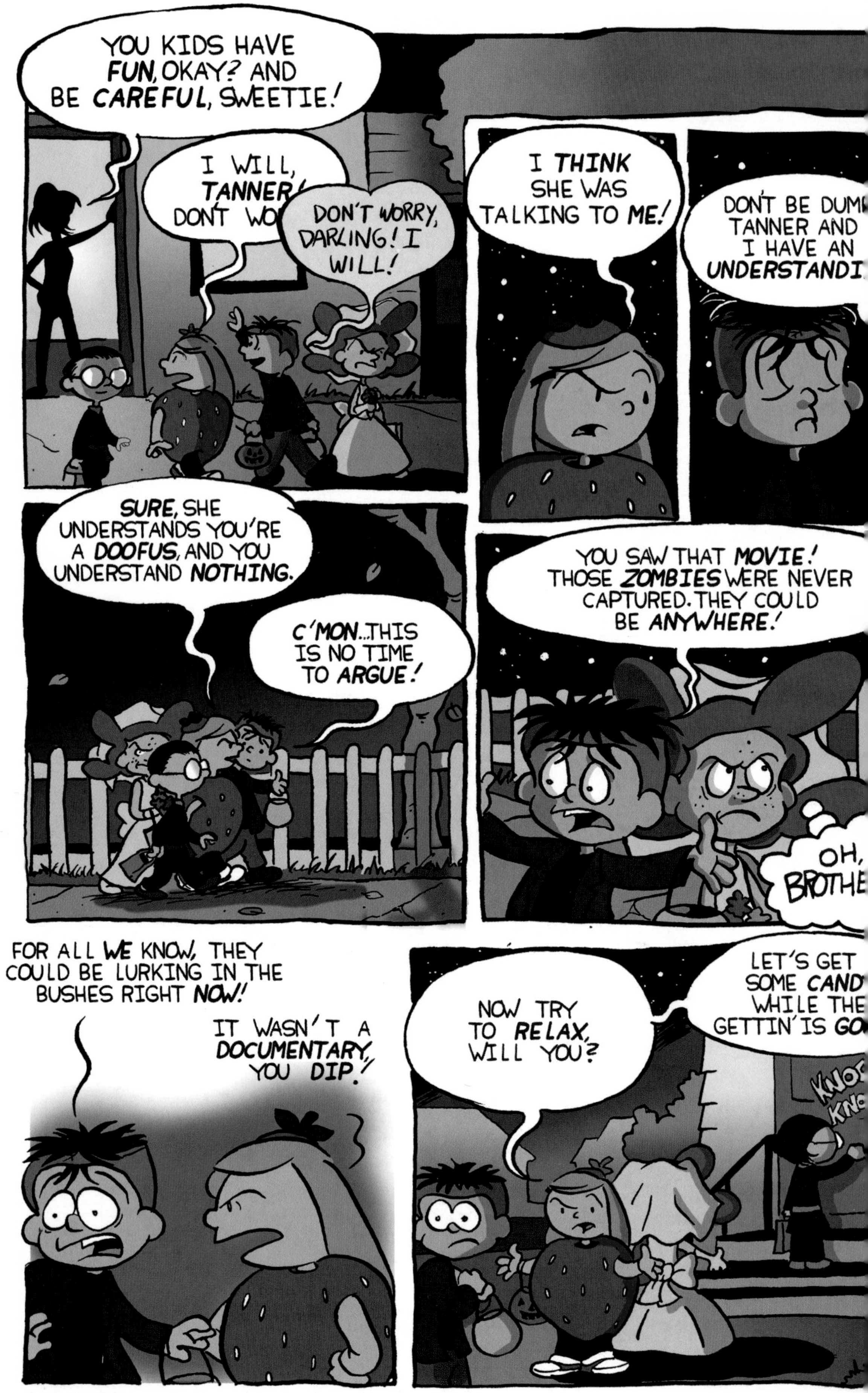

YOU KIDS HAVE FUN, OKAY? AND BE CAREFUL, SWEETIE!
I WILL, TANNER! DON'T WO
DON'T WORRY, DARLING! I WILL!
I THINK SHE WAS TALKING TO ME!
DON'T BE DUM TANNER AND I HAVE AN UNDERSTANDI
SURE, SHE UNDERSTANDS YOU'RE A DOOFUS, AND YOU UNDERSTAND NOTHING.
C'MON...THIS IS NO TIME TO ARGUE!
YOU SAW THAT MOVIE! THOSE ZOMBIES WERE NEVER CAPTURED. THEY COULD BE ANYWHERE!
OH, BROTHE
FOR ALL WE KNOW, THEY COULD BE LURKING IN THE BUSHES RIGHT NOW!
IT WASN'T A DOCUMENTARY, YOU DIP!
NOW TRY TO RELAX, WILL YOU?
LET'S GET SOME CAND WHILE THE GETTIN' IS GO

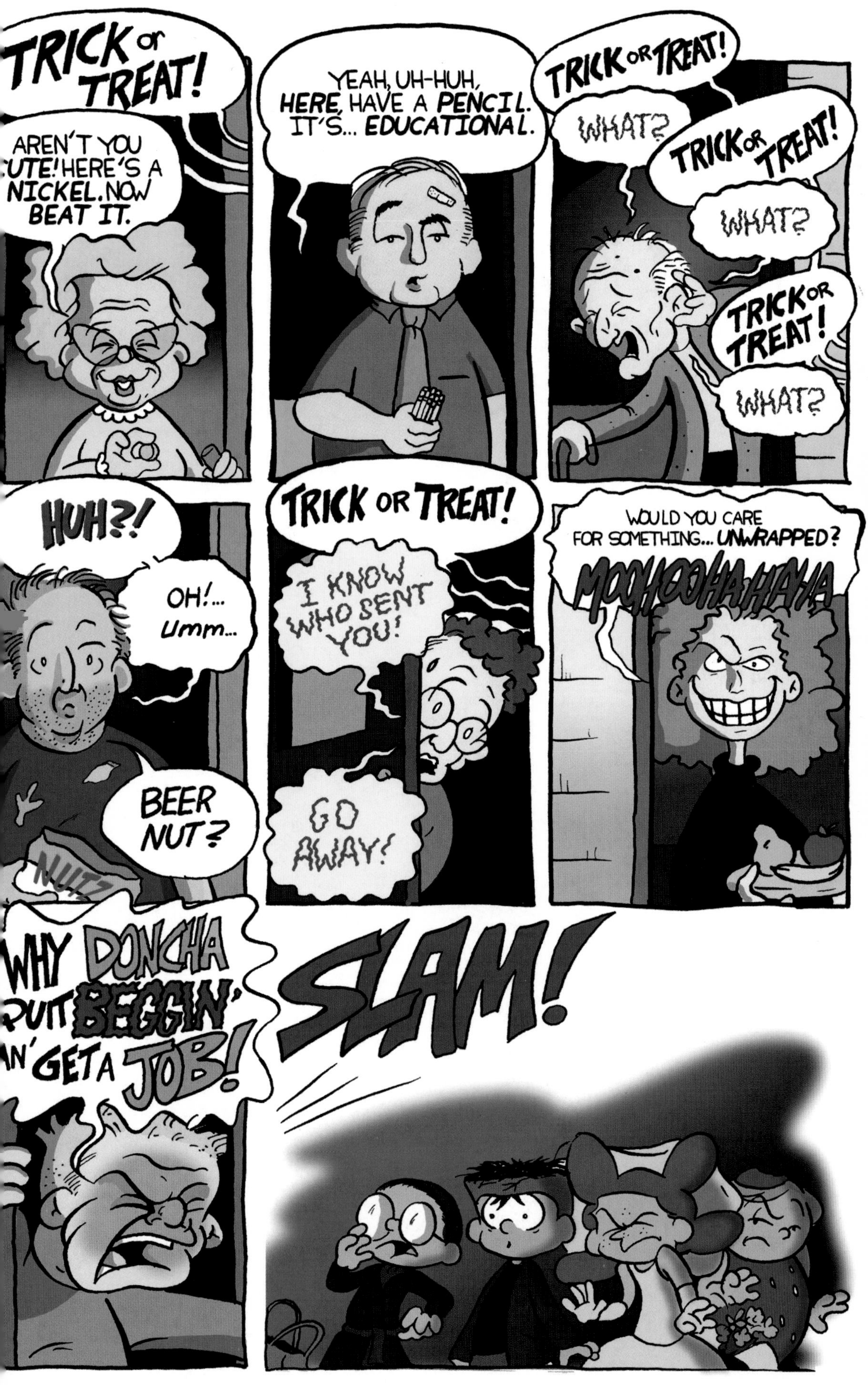
TRICK or TREAT!
AREN'T YOU CUTE! HERE'S A NICKEL. NOW BEAT IT.
YEAH, UH-HUH, HERE, HAVE A PENCIL. IT'S... EDUCATIONAL.
TRICK OR TREAT!
WHAT?
TRICK OR TREAT!
WHAT?
TRICK OR TREAT!
WHAT?
HUH?!
OH!... Umm...
BEER NUT?
NUTZ
TRICK OR TREAT!
I KNOW WHO SENT YOU!
GO AWAY!
WOULD YOU CARE FOR SOMETHING... UNWRAPPED?
MOOHOOHAHAHA
WHY DONCHA QUIT BEGGIN' AN' GET A JOB!
SLAM!

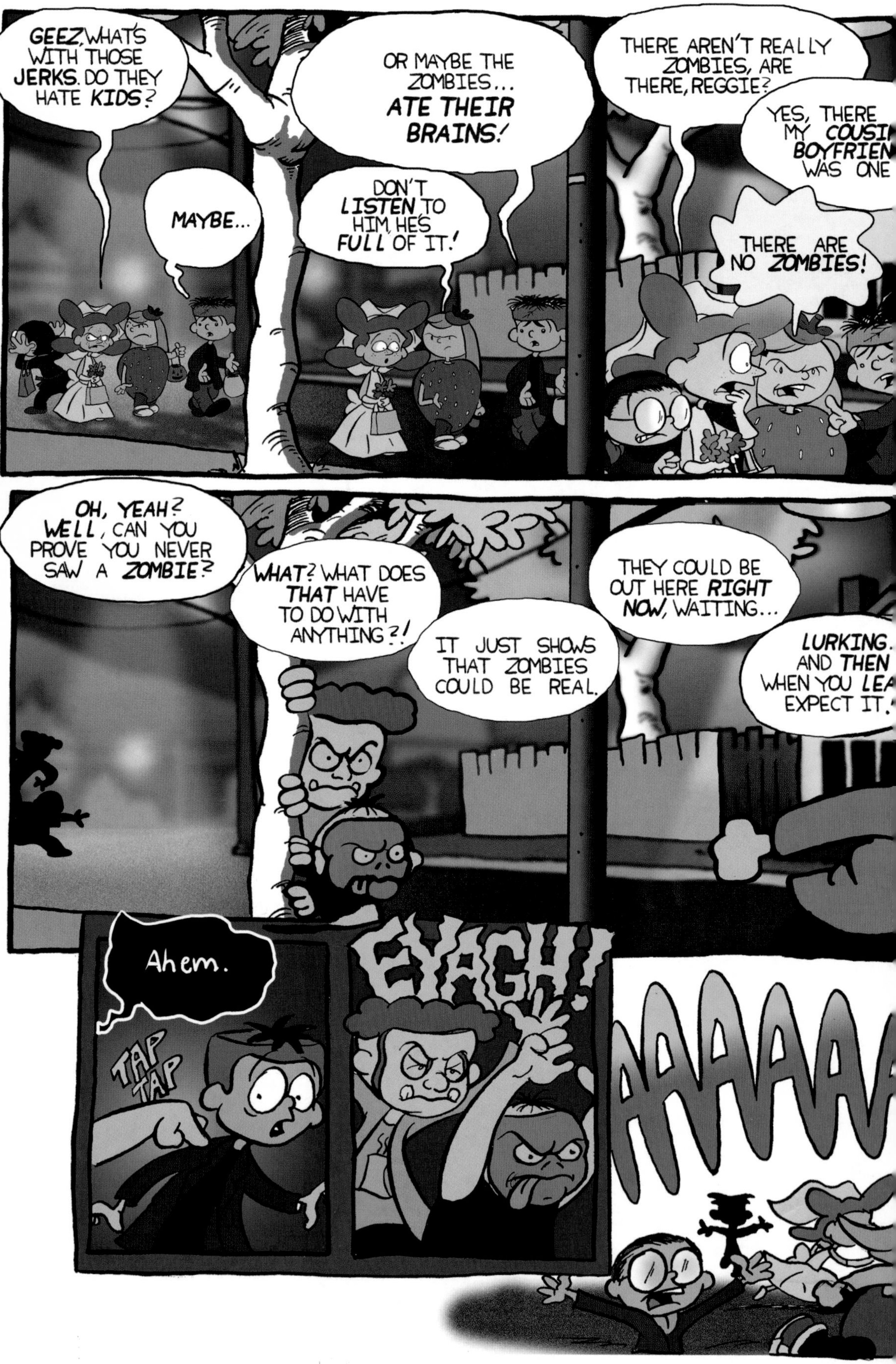
GEEZ, WHAT'S WITH THOSE JERKS. DO THEY HATE KIDS?
MAYBE...
OR MAYBE THE ZOMBIES... ATE THEIR BRAINS!
DON'T LISTEN TO HIM, HE'S FULL OF IT!
THERE AREN'T REALLY ZOMBIES, ARE THERE, REGGIE?
YES, THERE
MY
WAS ONE
THERE ARE NO ZOMBIES!
OH, YEAH? WELL, CAN YOU PROVE YOU NEVER SAW A ZOMBIE?
WHAT? WHAT DOES THAT HAVE TO DO WITH ANYTHING?!
IT JUST SHOWS THAT ZOMBIES COULD BE REAL.
THEY COULD BE OUT HERE RIGHT NOW, WAITING...
LURKING.
AND THEN
WHEN YOU
EXPECT IT.
Ahem.
TAP TAP
EYAGH!

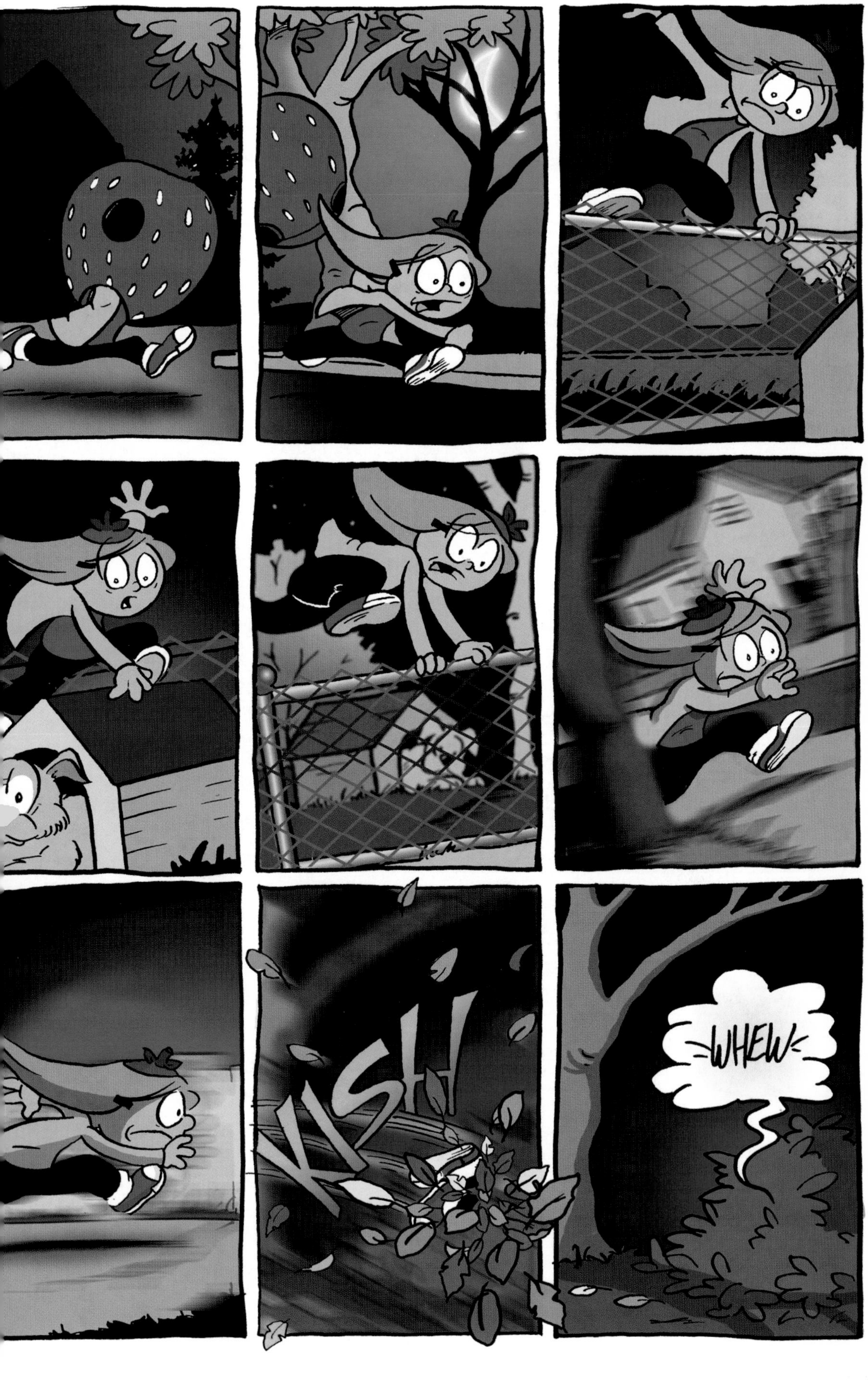
KISH
WHEW

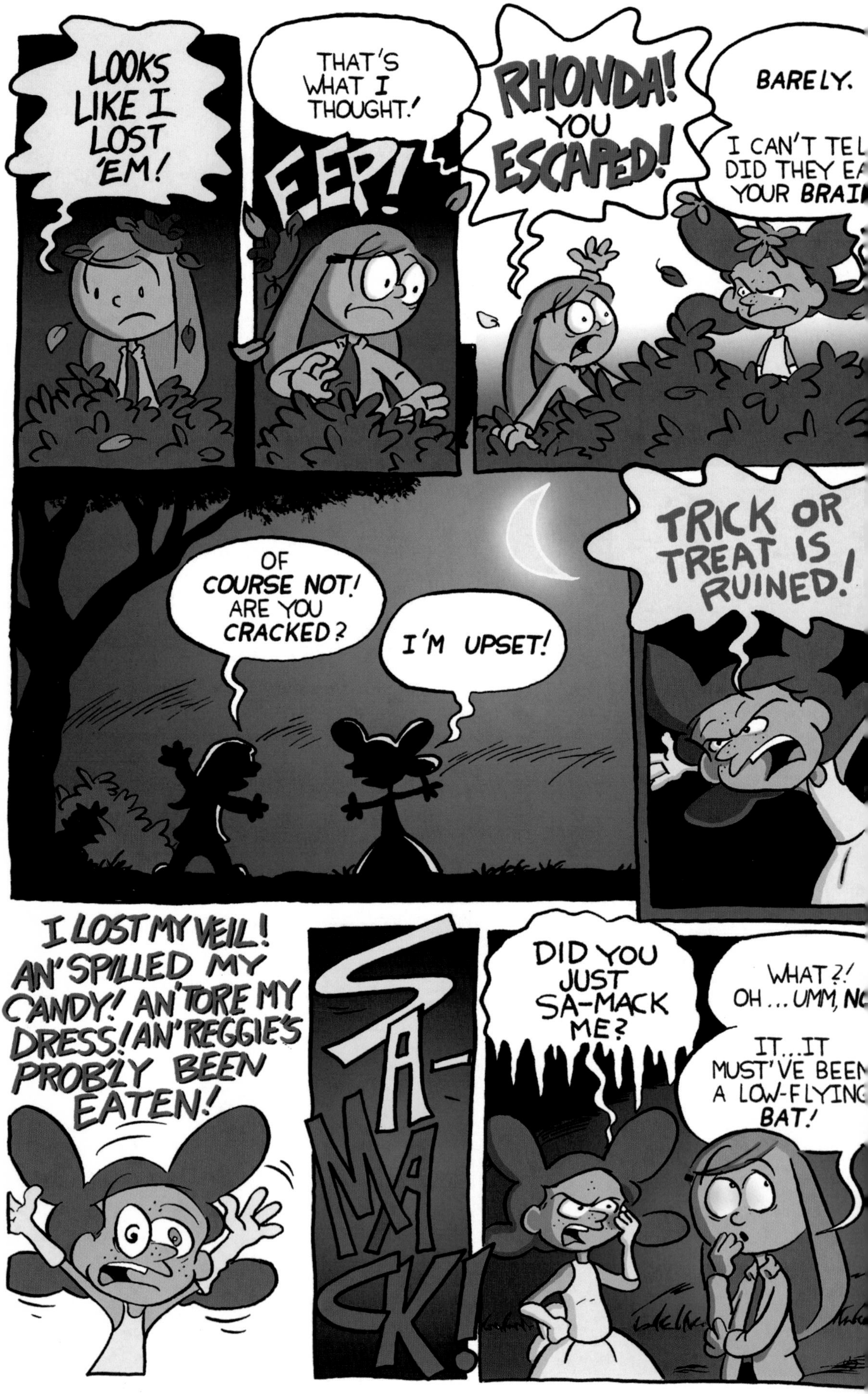
LOOKS LIKE I LOST 'EM!
THAT'S WHAT I THOUGHT!
EEP!
RHONDA! YOU ESCAPED!
BARELY.
I CAN'T TEL
DID THEY EA
YOUR BRAI
OF COURSE NOT! ARE YOU CRACKED?
I'M UPSET!
TRICK OR TREAT IS RUINED!
I LOST MY VEIL! AN' SPILLED MY CANDY! AN' TORE MY DRESS! AN' REGGIE'S PROB'LY BEEN EATEN!
SA-MACK!
DID YOU JUST SA-MACK ME?
WHAT?! OH...UMM, NO
IT...IT MUST'VE BEEN A LOW-FLYING BAT!

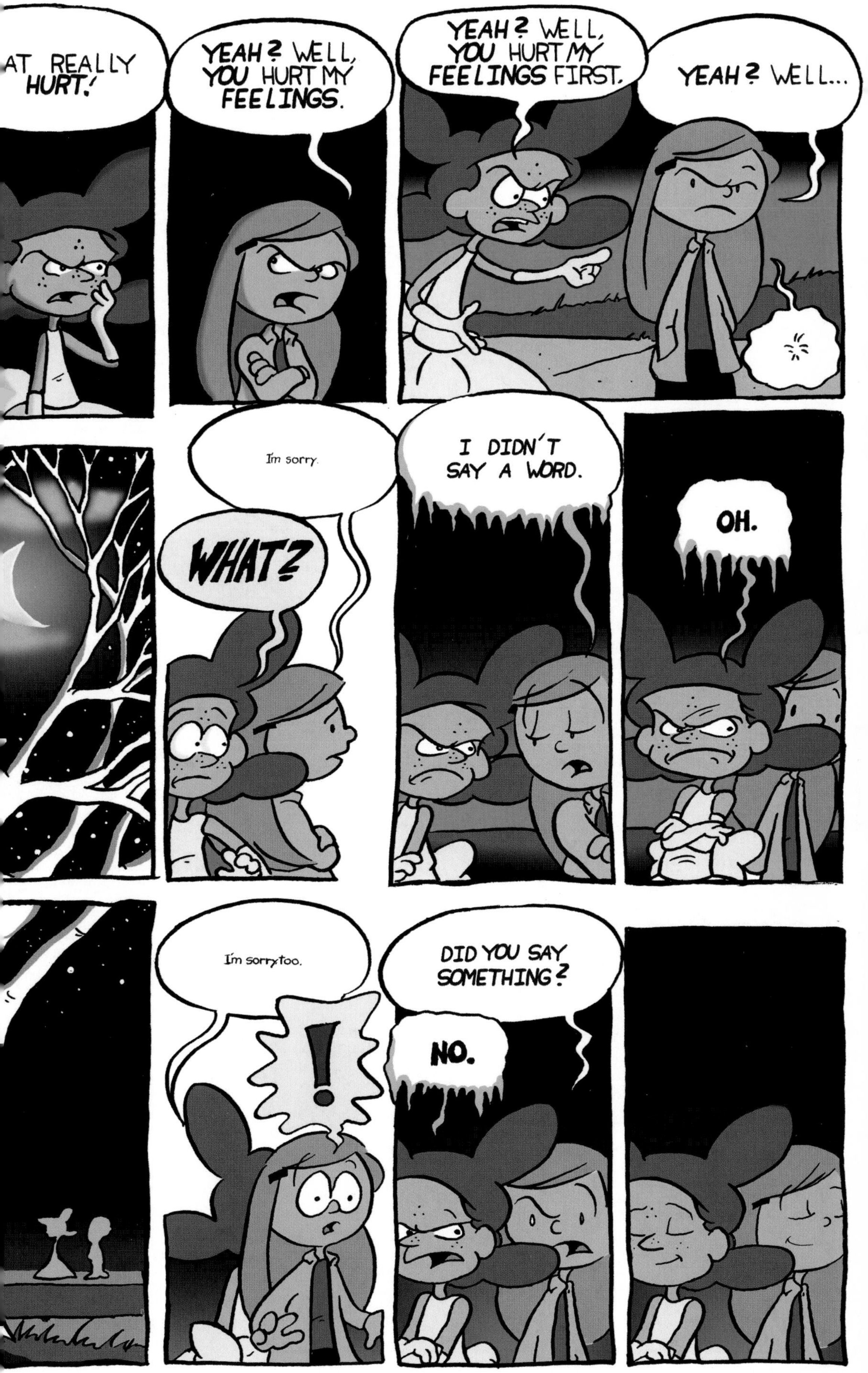

AT REALLY HURT!
YEAH? WELL, YOU HURT MY FEELINGS.
YEAH? WELL, YOU HURT MY FEELINGS FIRST.
YEAH? WELL...
I'm sorry.
WHAT?
I DIDN'T SAY A WORD.
OH.
I'm sorry too.
!
DID YOU SAY SOMETHING?
NO.

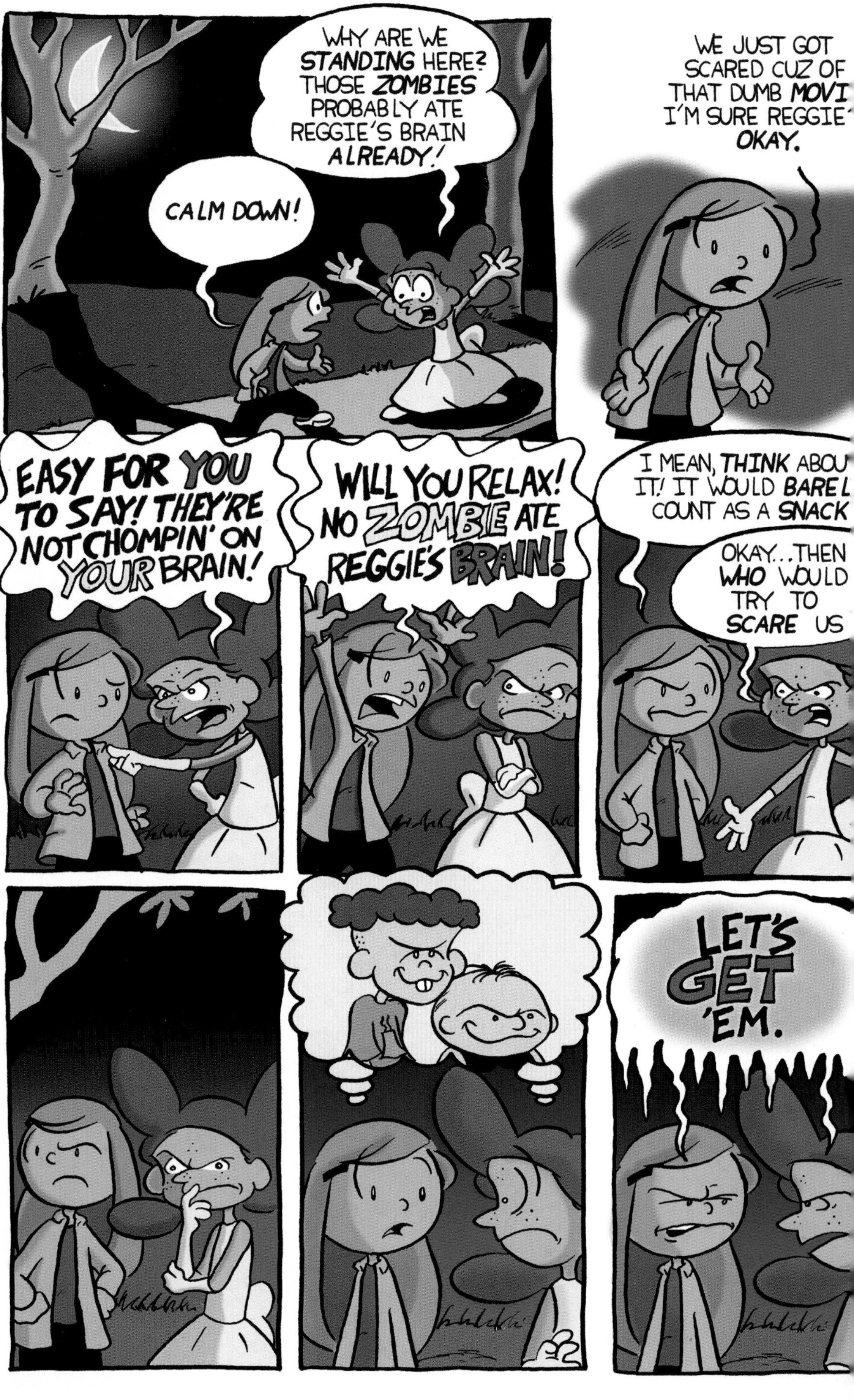

WHY ARE WE STANDING HERE? THOSE ZOMBIES PROBABLY ATE REGGIE'S BRAIN ALREADY!
CALM DOWN!
WE JUST GOT SCARED CUZ OF THAT DUMB MOVI I'M SURE REGGIE' OKAY.
EASY FOR YOU TO SAY! THEY'RE NOT CHOMPIN' ON YOUR BRAIN!
WILL YOU RELAX! NO ZOMBIE ATE REGGIE'S BRAIN!
I MEAN, THINK ABOU IT! IT WOULD BAREL COUNT AS A SNACK
OKAY...THEN WHO WOULD TRY TO SCARE US
LET'S GET 'EM.

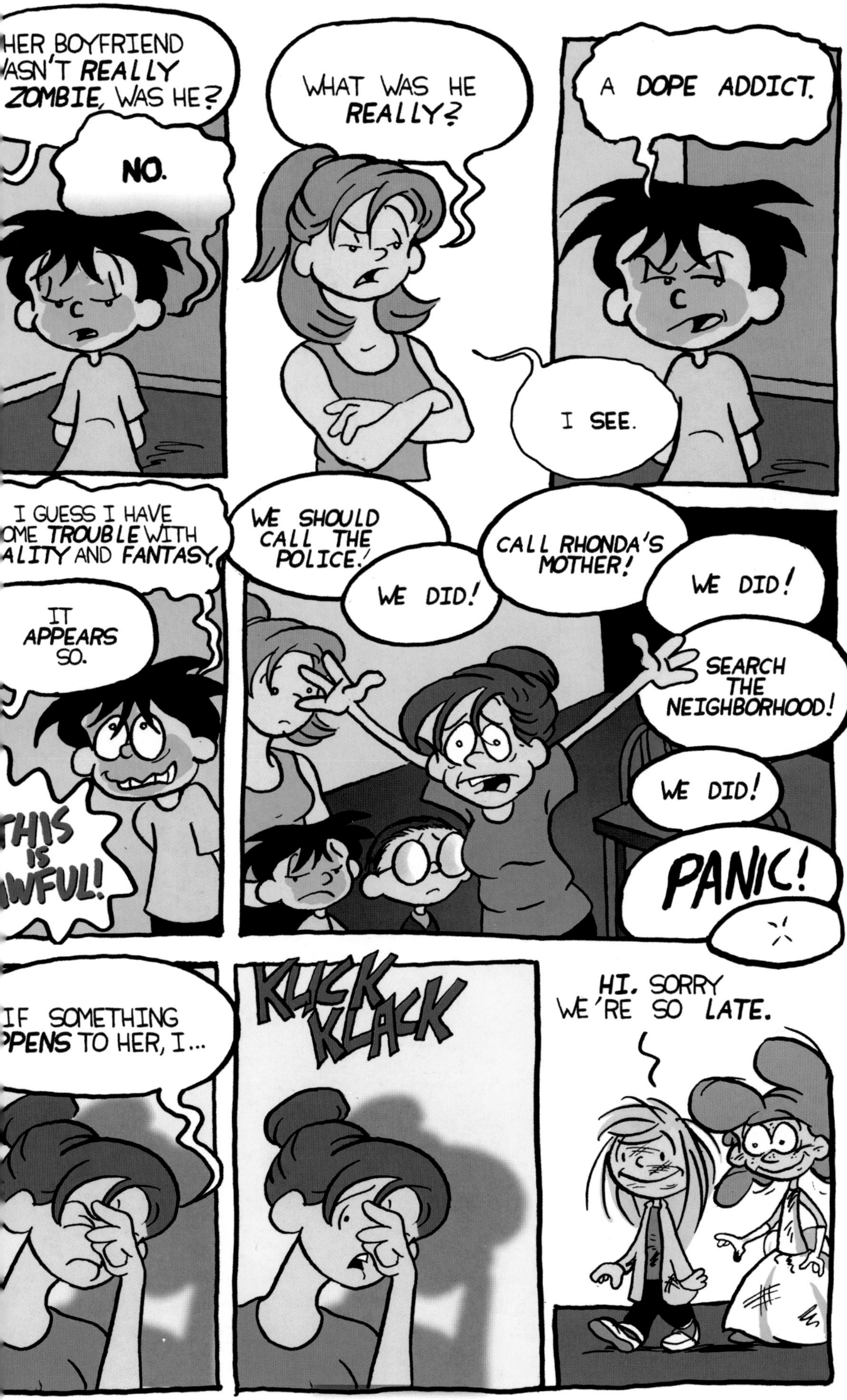

HER BOYFRIEND ASN'T REALLY ZOMBIE, WAS HE?
NO.
WHAT WAS HE REALLY?
A DOPE ADDICT.
I SEE.
I GUESS I HAVE OME TROUBLE WITH ALITY AND FANTASY.
IT APPEARS SO.
THIS IS WFUL!
WE SHOULD CALL THE POLICE!
WE DID!
CALL RHONDA'S MOTHER!
WE DID!
SEARCH THE NEIGHBORHOOD!
WE DID!
PANIC!
IF SOMETHING PPENS TO HER, I...
KLICK KLACK
HI. SORRY WE'RE SO LATE.

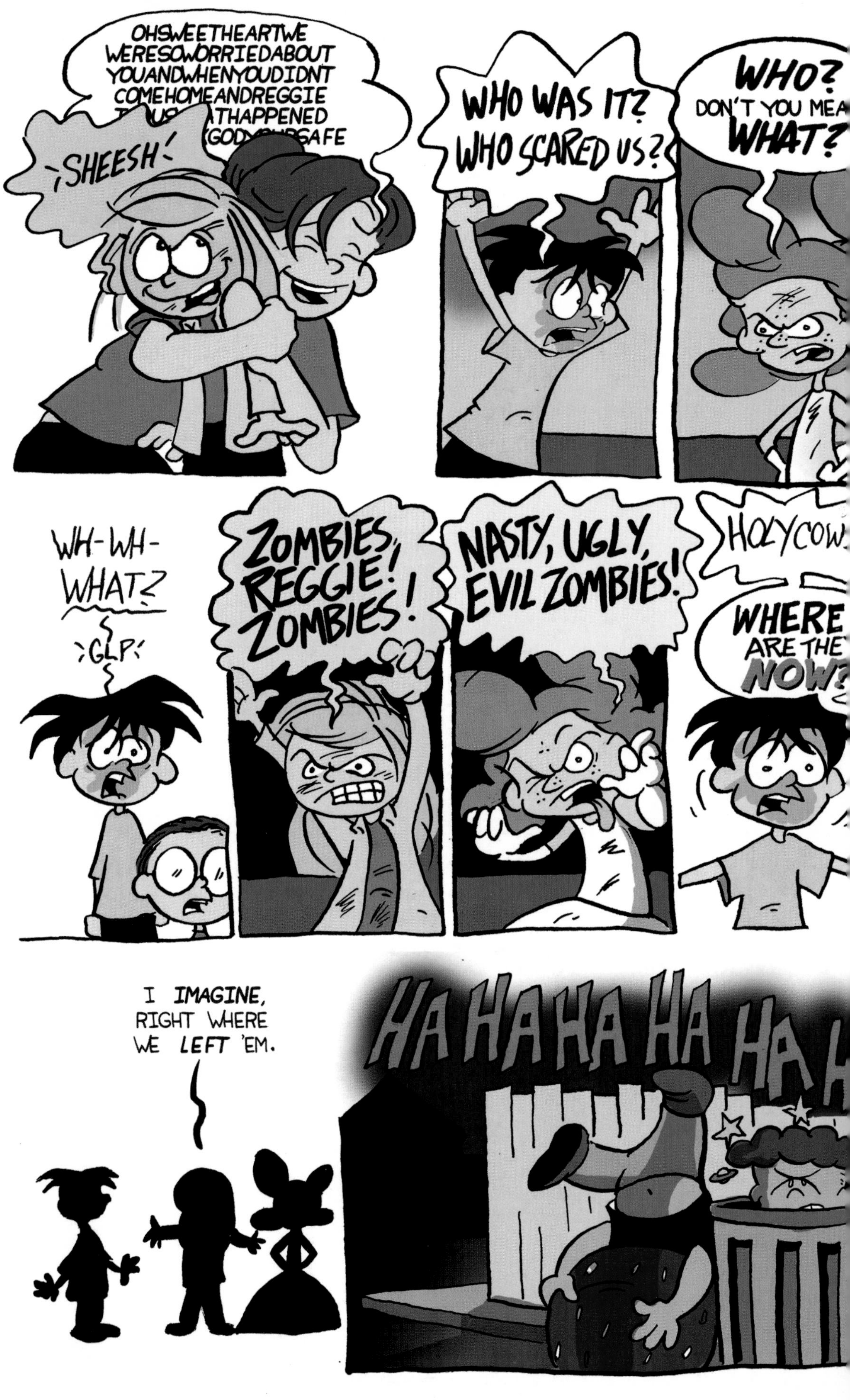

OHSWEETHEARTWE
WERESOWORRIEDABOUT
YOUANDWHENYOUDIDNT
COMEHOMEANDREGGIE
¡SHEESH!
WHO WAS IT? WHO SCARED US?
WHO? DON'T YOU MEA
WHAT?
WH-WH-WHAT?
GLP
ZOMBIES, REGGIE! ZOMBIES!
NASTY, UGLY, EVIL ZOMBIES!
HOLY COW
WHERE ARE THE
NOW?
I IMAGINE, RIGHT WHERE WE LEFT 'EM.
HA HA HA HA HA HA

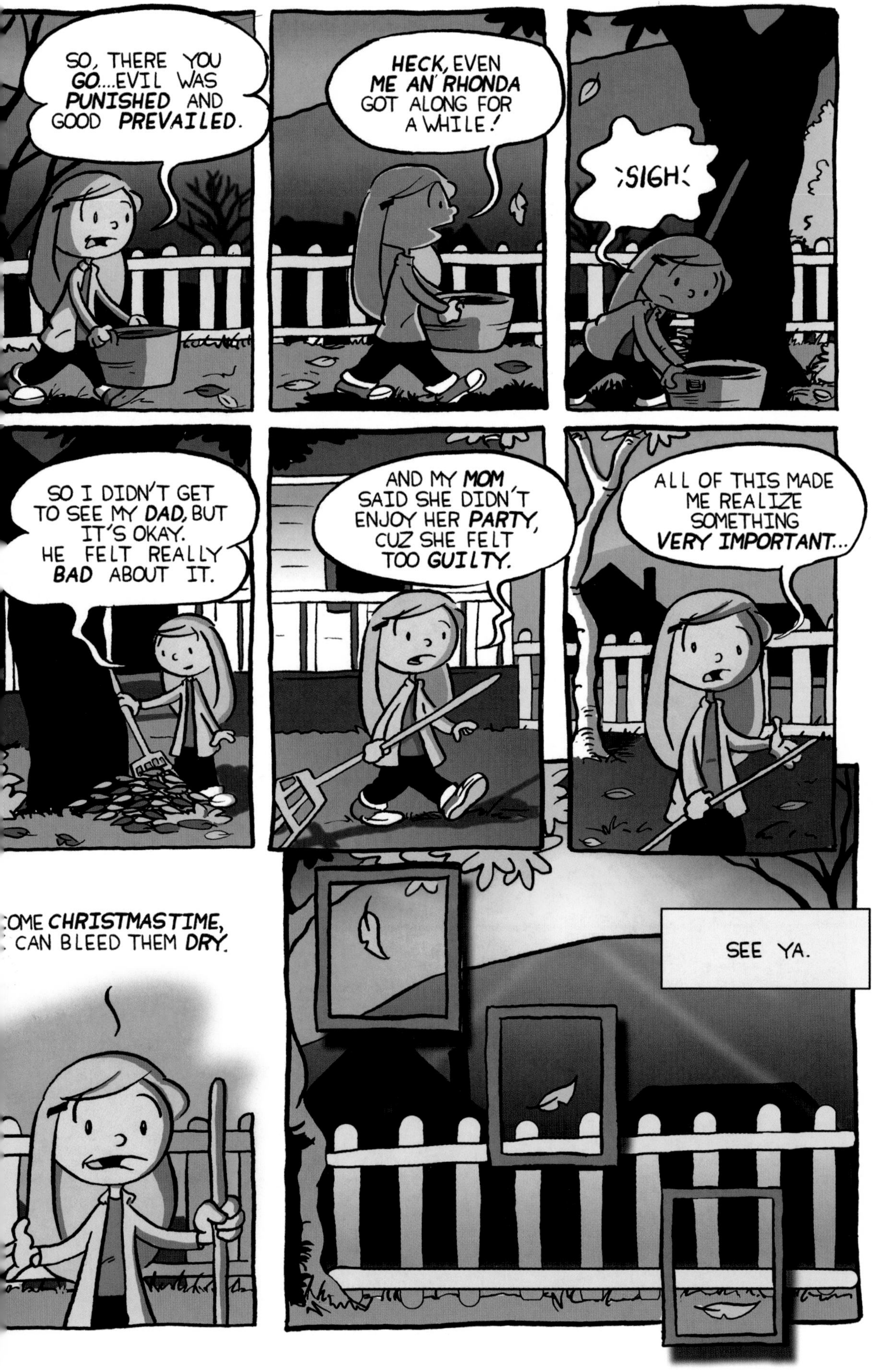
SO, THERE YOU GO....EVIL WAS PUNISHED AND GOOD PREVAILED.
HECK, EVEN ME AN' RHONDA GOT ALONG FOR A WHILE!
¡SIGH!
SO I DIDN'T GET TO SEE MY DAD, BUT IT'S OKAY. HE FELT REALLY BAD ABOUT IT.
AND MY MOM SAID SHE DIDN'T ENJOY HER PARTY, CUZ SHE FELT TOO GUILTY.
ALL OF THIS MADE ME REALIZE SOMETHING VERY IMPORTANT...
OME CHRISTMASTIME, CAN BLEED THEM DRY.
SEE YA.

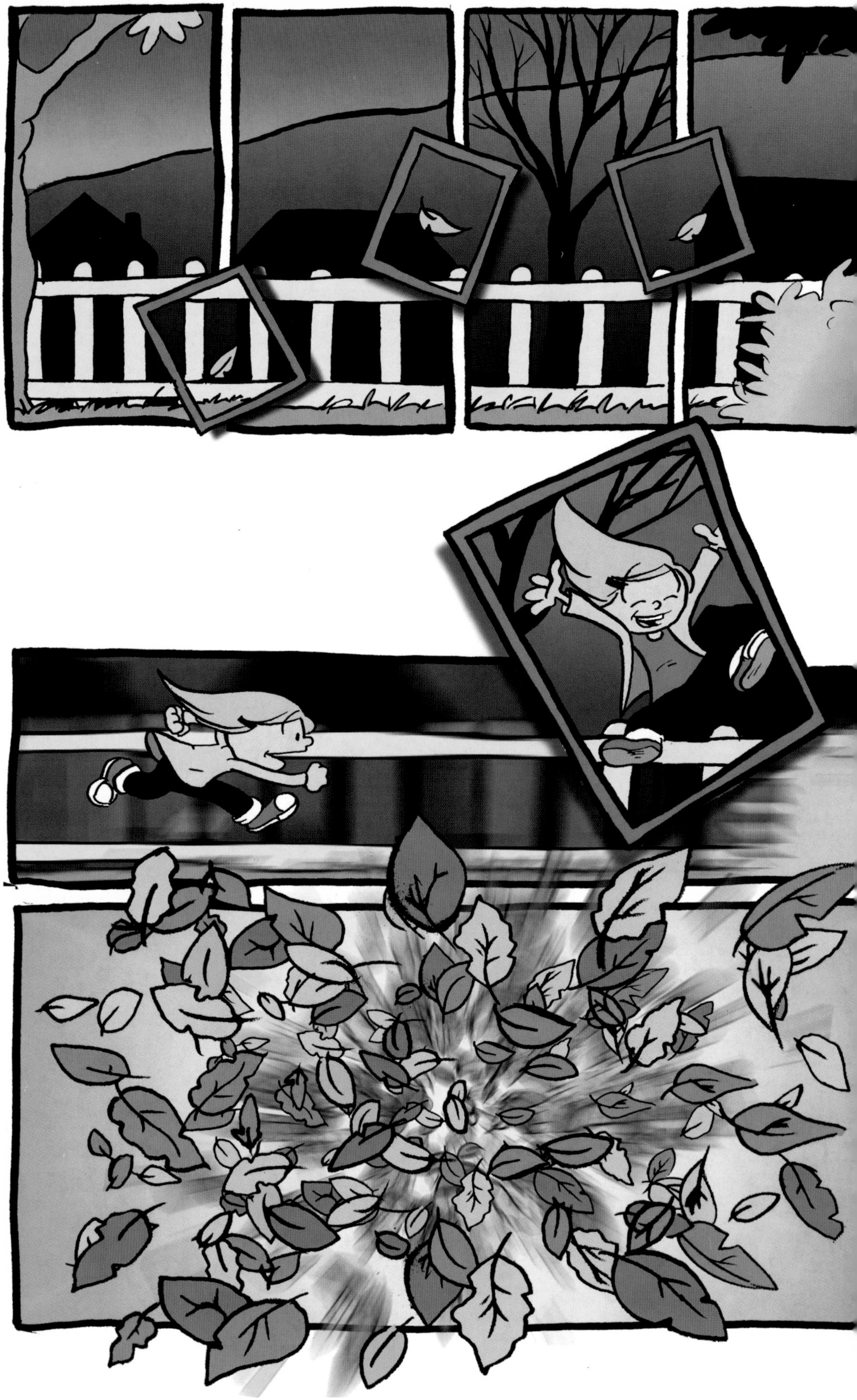